# An Angry Fix

Omar Haboubi

Copyright © Omar Haboubi 2013

Cover art by George Marsh

All rights reserved. No part of this publication may be reproduced, distributed or transmitted in any form or by any means, or stored in a database or retrieval system, without the prior written permission of the publisher.

ISBN: 1494241730
ISBN 13: 9781494241735

# Acknowledgments

I'd like to thank Wendy Toole for being my editor; Michael Heller, Sara Van Norman, Rob Curran, Paul Henry, Hayooma, The Prof, George Marsh and Richard Lyman for believing in my writing; and James Frey for reminding me that I could.

# Chapter 1

They got me good

I am moved outside. Legs, not working. Face, punch-numb. A number in my pocket. The scrawl says Dakota. They got me good tonight. I shouldn't have touched. I know that. But the truth is she grabbed me. Grabbed my hands, started moving them up and down. That should tell you all you need to know about me, about my luck. I'm always getting singled out, beaten on, always getting bullseyed for a whipping. Karma has a hard-on for old Huck.

I had walked in, past the big burly bone breakers—juicers just itching for a reason—paid my entrance, politely ordered a bourbon. A few rounds later, I was getting oiled up, and trying to cultivate a bit of privacy, when everything started to tornado, engulfing me in its naked, self-loathing madness. In its venereal prostitution. I hated these places. But I came a lot. City brothels, filthily milling out questions as directives. Destroying you with them. *Buy me a drink, buy yourself a dance, another drink, mind if I sit down? THAT'S TWENTY DOLLARS.* Let me save you some money, if you don't already know, aren't wise to it: if you want somewhere to sit, wait, brood, if you want somewhere to regret and better yourself, a strip club is the wrong joint. There is no nursing your drink, killing time. There is only twenty dollars a button. They take your finger, press it for you. Then repeat. And more when you're in blackout. I've seen continents of wealth swiped clean away from the unconscious. That's why I keep my credit card in my shoe, and pay for everything in cash.

Head resting on sidewalk, everything spinning (I've been at it heavy, even for me), left eye closed, right on taxi detail, I need an escape from my current mess. (Just so you know, that's how it is with me: new ground, becomes current mess, requires a taxi, to new ground, becomes more mess, and on and on. Taxis are how I deal.) I hustle to my feet, trying my best to look like a citizen, flag a ride. It doesn't appear to be working too well. Not today. A hundred yellows fly by, ignoring my hands, my obvious need. At last, one takes pity, unlocks his doors, takes my address.

Safely tucked up in the back, I try closing my eyes, catch a little shut-eye, but the spinning picks up speed and almost lands me in trouble. I open them just in time to save myself extra for the cleanup. I am known for vomiting in cabs. Among other things, that is what I am known for. And fighting. On the North side of Chicago, I am known as an aggressive, shitty brawler.

The driver pulls up to my apartment, quotes me a fare. I reach into my pocket. Aside from my cell phone, cigarettes, keys and Dakota's number, I have nothing. I wonder where all the money went. I must have had a hell of a time. I clap my hands together to get the driver's attention.

"Look here, friend, I'm not going to insult you and tell you I have the money. The truth is I had a bunch of it, loads of it, probably enough for a hundred taxis, but somehow and along the way I've managed to blow it all. Maybe I got a hand job out of it, maybe I didn't, I don't want to speculate. A girl called Dakota, she might know. Anyway, all that's beside the point. What I'm trying to say is: let's work this out the old-fashioned way, like men. Forget calling the police. The fucking paperwork makes them edgy."

So here I am: outside my apartment, me swinging wildly, trying to land the sleeper.

The driver is old school, pure technique. Sticking and moving, jabbing. Lots of jabbing. Skin splits, blood pours, eyes close. He punishes me bad. He turns on the style and really lays it on me. You should know, I have a knack for that. For picking fights with natural fighters. From down on the floor, wheezing, through what I'm certain is a punctured lung, I see him smiling. He's got his money's worth, *double* probably. I try smiling back, but my lip's busted, and I can't. I start coughing, coughing up a storm. "You okay?" he says. "Fine," I say. It would be good to be able to fight. Properly, I mean. It would be nice to feel more involved—in the fighting process. I make a mental note to learn, maybe take some private classes.

Three in the morning, I enter the house. A letter from Lipton has been slipped under my door. *Not tonight.* I put it to the side. I make straight for the painkillers, double dose. It's five, and the birds are taunting, pecking away at my spirit. Each chirp punches into the middles of my brain. The pills have done their work, numbed my left eye, giving me one pain-free screwed-up socket. I try to think of anything else, anything aside from my left eye, that I'm okay with. I decide no. And like always I think about "the other thing"—you know, about hitting the goodbye button, flicking the sayonara switch. Just thoughts though. No razorblades. Not tonight, not tonight, no razorblades, not tonight. I fade out.

I wake up, still on the bathroom floor, curled up with a glass of lemonade and a cheese sandwich, half-eaten and placed on the tile next to my left cheek. I check my watch. It says nine. Somewhere in the four-hour blackout, I must have gotten up and made myself something to eat. I'm good like that. I have a blackout work ethic. Not a lot drunks can say that. I think it's because if I didn't I wouldn't get things done, meaning I wouldn't survive, wouldn't exist. I look around for the plate. No plate. I try to get up, using the toilet bowl for leverage, but my legs aren't cooperating, and I fall back down, hitting my head on the porcelain. Unable to take another beating, I stay down. I drain the lemonade, and it's not enough, and I try to flush the cheese sandwich, but it doesn't go down. I watch it a while. Watch the bread bloat, break, float on the surface. And fetal position, eyes closed, I pass out again.

## Purple means blood

Two days later. I've picked myself up, and had one of my *fatal recollections*. The kind I get when I come out of a drunk, and remember what I'd planned on doing, before booze got me sidetracked. Like turning up to a first date. I'd made one, but missed it, meaning that needed cleaning up. I drag myself into less-stained clothes, dunk my head in a basin of ice-water (to cool the sickness off me). Then I exit my apartment, and flag a cab.

"There were three of them," I say, "black guys."
 So here I am, lying again. And although it's to a new girl—meaning one who doesn't know my

bullshit *personally*—I'm still nervous. That's because *every* woman, by the age of sixteen, has been dumped on enough times (by guys like me) to have formed a general suspicion against men. Meaning, even if you come at them with perfectly acted sincerity and well-manicured lies, the chances of them buying what you're selling is at best a coin toss.

"I didn't want to mention that they were colored. What with racial profiling being the way it is. But they *were* black. And they *did* snatch the white lady's purse. And there's no escaping the facts. Even when they *do* leave a bad taste in your mouth."

This girl—a waitress called Rumi—isn't saying anything. Not a goddamn word. She's just studying me, eye-grinding, cranking up the pressure. Making me sweat like a rapist.

"The point is," I say, "I *had* to fight them. Even if it meant getting beaten up and missing our date."

Obviously, I can't tell her the truth: that I'd missed our date because I'm an alcoholic. And I've difficulty staying sober enough to remember plans. But defending a woman, outnumbered three to one? She'd have to be twisted not to like that, to get off on it even. Of course, I have to sell it first. And my sweat-dripping, voice-shaking, eyes-shifting isn't helping.

"So that's why you didn't show?"

I don't say anything. Instead, I point to the bruises. The ones on my face. Then I lift up my shirt. I show her the purple banana across my ribs: the cab driver's work.

"They did that to you?"

She brushes her fingers across my side. There is no pain. It looks bad, but only because I bruise easy. Still, I take the opportunity to wince, clutch the bruising, squeeze my eyes.

"Shit," she says.

"It looks worse than it is." I make a half-turn, giving her a full showing of the purple, hoping she knows that means blood under the surface.

"Did you file a report?"

"The police?" I suck in air like an old person. "There's not much *they* can do. I'm not saying it's their fault," I say. "No, I blame the system."

Let me tell you about the system. I use it a lot, lay things on its doorstep a bunch. Everyone understands the system, understands getting beaten up, picked on, singled out, fucked over.

She studies me some more, but thankfully not for too long, before nodding her head.

"All right," she says, "meet me here at eleven." She checks her watch and frowns. "I got to get back."


I pocket the card

I've got a couple of hours to kill before eleven. So a few Valium, to smooth things out, and off I go in search of somewhere to kill time. I pass a couple of bars. But they're not for me. They're places I've caused bother, broken things, probably owe some money. So I give them a miss. I step into the road and force a cab to pull over. I climb in and hand over the name of a place, a snooty four-room box, up in the Gold Coast. It's a hard-to-find, and cool-because-of-it, hole, stinky with pretension. I hate this place, and all places like it. There's nothing worker-bee about them, nothing honest. They're a stopgap for bankers, lawyers, for legal thieves (the big robbers) itching to scratch a dirty itch.

I enter, sit down, order myself two fancy beers with silly names, and set my alarm for ten thirty. I look around. It's too early for the real animals, but already the place is peppered with yawning girls—heads sitting on rib cages, sitting on stilts, sitting on five-hundred-dollar heels—sniffing out the good bets. Yes, yes, I know: I loathe this joint, yet here I am. *Because* I'll be safe here. With beers, bad company, I will not get carried away, I will not lose myself in a good time, and miss my second shot.

A bloody-nosed emaciation comes over to the bar. She sits down—next to me, but almost on my lap. She asks if I'd like to buy her a drink. I close my eyes. The answer is no, yes, no... back and forth. Because she is annoying. Because she is hot. My problem is I am weak. I'm not good at stopping when I need to: at flirting. I see a light, I see green, I take it too far, I get slapped, or worse.

That's my M.O. My downstairs runs things, gets me into all sorts of trouble. But when I turn she's gone. Probably looking for a better benefactor.

I finish the bottles, pick up the menu, choose a country. The Sudan. Even though the menu says otherwise, I'm almost certain they don't make beer over there. I call the bartender over, and order two. I know I'll be sober on beers—yellow, fizzy water. I know I'll be dry, bored, awake. I know I will keep my mind right. I glue my eyes to my wrist. I watch the second hand. I avoid the erupting bustle, the co-mingling of importantly chic, chiseled, gaunt, with the aging, gut-hanging, chauffeured, fat-dripping moneyed types. I take another sip, disgusted. Look at them: oiled prostitutes and the vinegared rich—them that need to pay, and them that demand payment. It's not the prostitution that upsets me. Hell, everyone sells something to get by. It's the not calling it what it is—that's what gets to me—the nineteen-year-old marrying the sixty-year-old for "love," the sixty-year-old marrying his could-be granddaughter for "companionship."

"Change your mind?"

The clothes rack from a minute ago is back from the toilet—from a nose job, from powdering her nose—and she is pressing me. It's the cocaine. Women do that on coke. They act like men. They get all belligerent. That's not for me, that kind of obviousness, so I ignore her. She handles the small of my back. She does it like a pro, her fingernails trailing, suggestively.

"About buying me a drink," she says.

I don't want any trouble tonight. Tonight I want to make my date.

"I never considered paying for your company."

Ignoring my fuck-you, she tells me that she likes me.

I want to buy her a drink. Ten drinks. I want to take her home, to the toilets, to the alleyway. What I *really* want is to tie her up. I want to break some laws. Some big greasy laws.

"Look," I say, "you don't like me."

"How do you know?"

"Because you don't know me."

"Yes," she says, starting up again with the fingernails, "that could be why I do."

"What's your game?"

"No game. Just thought you looked okay."

"Well I'm not."

"Buy me a drink."

"I'm engaged."

I am not engaged. I will never be engaged. I think marriage is for suckers. For people committed to not getting ahead.

"Liar."

"I am," I say, "and she's the jealous type." I raise my shirt. "Purple means internal bleeding."

"Your wife did that to you?"

"Fiancée."

"Kids?"

"What?"

"You have kids?"

"Look," I say, "I'm not being rude..." I point for her to leave, but she remains where she is.

"You're full of it," she says.

"Excuse me?"

"I said: you're full of *shit*."

She's right, of course. But I wonder how she knows. I must ooze it. It must be coming off me something rotten, like a stink, like an obvious stench.

"If I'm right"—she slides across a card—"then call me... But not if you really *do* have kids." She stands up, adjusts her tights. Brilliant legs. I can feel a rise. "I can't stand the little shits."

And with that she's gone. Peach hair, velvet skin, eyes emerald.

I pocket the card.


## Drinks, The Conversation

I do not use the card. Not that night. Instead, I stick it in my pocket. I sit and sip and finish my beer, then drink another, and another, and more, but only beers. And I make my date. Then more drinks, proper drinks this time, with the waitress. And I'm on fine form. I make her laugh. She has a nice laugh. I like hearing it, like knowing that I did that. I forgot I could be funny. I've been kind of serious for a while now, really in the dumps, depressed. She turns to me, once we're deep in the swirl, once we're half-blind, and slurring, and sexual. And she tells me she has a small mattress. She blushes. "Not many guys know that." She's indicating that she doesn't sleep around, that her offering herself to me makes me special. She takes my hand and we take a cab and no one throws up in the back and we go back to hers and no one throws up at hers and we have sex and no one throws up. And it's nice. And she passes out. And I lie there. I don't sleep too good, so I think, because I think a lot, until it gets light, then I stop thinking and pass out. And when we awake, she smiles at me, like she's not embarrassed, so I smile back, because I'm not embarrassed, and we go out for breakfast and it feels good and not forced and I tell her all about the book I'm writing. How I'm writing it. And the creative process. Then I tell her all about Kafka. She seems interested in what I have to say. She is a good listener. She asks questions. Like if all writers are tragic. She says she's a small town girl, and just a waitress and she doesn't know these things, and she apologizes. She is embarrassed and it is endearing. I tell her not to be embarrassed. And I tell her yes. All writers are tragic. "Even you?" she asks. "Even me," I say. "You're sad?" she says. I nod. She says she's sorry. And we have more drinks. She's not working for two days so after breakfast we go out for drinks. For two days. We drink for two days after breakfast. And it's nice. I need a woman who drinks. A woman who drinks like me. A woman who will not judge how much I drink. She has lots of questions about my book. And it's hard keeping the lies straight. So in the end I tell her I don't want to talk about it. That makes her sad. And that, making her sad, makes me sad. So I drink. And she drinks. And we both talk less, and drink the same, maybe I drink a little more. But I'm bigger, and not much more. And not enough to make a difference. Not enough to let her judge me. We don't talk much, and we have sex. A lot of sex. From really late to really early. After her shift we go at it for hours. Mouths everywhere, flesh everywhere, rolling around. I take to sleeping at hers, and do so every night, save two, over the next four weeks. Last night we had "the conversation" so now we're officially an item. I like that. I like that she is my girl.

Some girls get sloppy. It normally takes about a month for them to stop putting the effort in. Then they start slipping, start acting loose. I dated this one girl, a real girly girl, until we got about a month in. Then she started belching, farting up a storm, taking dumps with the door open. I mean, Christ. Masculine women slay me. They kill me in the downstairs. I couldn't fuck her after that.

As hot as she was, I just couldn't get the engine running. I dated this other girl who was perfect. Smart, funny, hot, tight, clever, considerate, beautiful feet. She had it all. Until a month in. Until I took a look at her hands. Not just a cursory glance to make sure she was holding ten. No, I mean, like a proper investigation of her knuckles to tips. I found this one loose hair on her right index finger. A big curly dirty number. It was the most disgusting thing I'd ever seen. So I had to end it. Then I met this other girl. And she was great. Except she had big feet. I couldn't deal with that. I like small feet, dainty feet, doll's feet, Chinese feet. So I had to sit her down. Then another girl, her problem was that she snored, and not in a cute way either, but a proper wake-you-up, old man horn. There were other girls too. Other deal-breakers... I hope you're getting my point. It's not that I want to be alone. No, no it's not that. But it's karma, man, it has me noticing things. It points out line-crossers, then rubs them in my face. Karma, I'm telling you, *karma* has a hard-on for me. Like it *needs* me to be lonely. Like it feeds off it.

But right now I don't feel lonely. Not with this girl. No, this girl is perfect. Without getting into it, I really feel like, well, like I could be, you know what I'm trying to say... I've stopped going to strip clubs, stopped feeling their pull. That's how I know. We hit two months and I couldn't be happier. I think about saying the words. I've never said them before. But I'm honestly considering it.

## Done

It's a normal day. She heads off to work. I am in love. I head back to mine. I can only shower at hers. I like to take long baths, do some thinking, but she's lost the plug, so I head back to mine. I have a nicer apartment—hers is a shoebox with cockroaches and other creepy crawlies—but she's funny about sleeping over so we always stay at hers. On her small mattress. Watch TV, eat hotbox pizza, fuck, laugh. We both find the same things funny, we're both into observational humor. So normally I meet her at the diner, after her shift, then go back to hers. But the day I spend at mine, getting drunk, taking baths, listening to records, not writing. And today is a day like the other days. Today is a normal day.

I am in the bath. I hear noises. Fuck. I must have left the door open. *A man is here. He has come to kill me.* My bones freeze. I'd checked the door, and rechecked, and kept rechecking to make sure my checking was right. I have big time OCD. Somehow I must have fucked up though. Because I can hear him, tiptoeing about real quiet.

Let me tell you about OCD... In fact, let me ask you this: Have you ever done that? Done what I've just done? Checked something four times, and by the fourth time you know you've checked it at least once, but then for some reason this thing inside you, this driving force, gets you to check again, even though you don't want to? And when you're sure you've checked it enough, you leave it alone. But then after a while you start to doubt all your checks and rechecks. So you check again. Have you ever done that? Well that's OCD. It's hard work. It adds to "the cloud." Have I told you about "the cloud"? That's what I call my sadness. I call it "the cloud" because that's what it is. This big mass of grayness, hovering over me, following me around, making everything seem drab and pointless and dull and dark. It's been around for forever (I had a tough childhood), but it's gotten worse since I got my inheritance, quit my job...

*He's in the hall. I'm sure of it.* I keep the water turned off for the longest time, my ears pricked, tuned in for a pin-drop. Nothing. He knows I'm listening so he's staying perfectly still. I psych myself up, slam my head into the wall a few times just to get the blood going, and then, courage up, I climb out of the bath and creep around the apartment, like an intruder, dripping soap, knife in hand, ready to stab, and keep stabbing. (It started three months ago—keeping a knife at hand. It began innocently enough, with just one, under my bed. Now

I keep them in the kitchen—on top of the fridge; in the bathroom—by the side of the sink; and in the living room—down the back of the couch.) The locks haven't been tampered with. Everything is secure. Everything is always secure and the locks have never been picked, and that surprises me every time. On the way back to the bathroom I fall on the wet floor, bang my head on the corner of the hall table, on metal. Head throbbing, bleeding too, I rinse off and lie down. I know falling asleep after a head injury is dangerous. But I'm feeling kind of dizzy, so I let myself pass out. I am always doing stuff like that. Banging my head on purpose. Banging my head by accident. This is a normal day.

Ever have your entire world come crashing down? That ever happen? And I don't mean, do you know someone it's happened to? I mean, has it ever happened *to you*? Because if not then you'll have no idea what it feels like next.

I never thought I'd fall—in love. With drugs, with booze, sure. But not with a person. Not really. As a rule, if I'm with a girl it's only because I've managed to curb all my natural impulses to run. And I can only manage that for about a month. Then it's "we need to talk." I've never been told that, never heard "we need to talk." Not once. I am always the runner.

I go to the diner to pick her up. And everything's the same, same as normal. On the way back she tells me about her day—her co-workers, her stupid manager, the funny things that happened, the good customers, the rude customers—same as normal. We get back to hers. She says we need to have a chat. "Cool," I say, and sit down. I like having chats with Rumi, but when we sit down she looks, I don't know, edgy, and she's not normally like that. So I take her hand, because, you know, I love her, but she pulls away.

"I don't think you're a writer, Huck."

"I love you."

"You keep saying you're a writer—"

"I *am* a writer. I love you."

"But I haven't seen you write a thing."

"I love you."

"In fact, I haven't seen *anything* you've written."

"I—"

"Do you know, I doubt very much you've even read Kafka, or if you have, you've read one book, maybe not even that, maybe you just know some lines, quotes to make you look clever. But *you* know you haven't read him, and you hate yourself for it. Well... now you know I know..."

"Look—"

"I can't be with someone who lies to me," she says. "It's over."

I feel like crying. I feel like crying hard. I feel like getting on my knees, and begging her not to do this. But I know girls. I know what they go for. And what turns them off. So I keep my feelings to myself. Instead I stare at her, blankly. I stare at her like she stares at me. If this was a movie, the screen would show two strangers in a filthy shoebox room, staring.

"Look, this is for you." She hands me an envelope. I take it. "Don't read it until you get home," she says.

"Okay," I say.

"Please go home," she says.

There's not much I can say after that, so I say nothing. I stand up, pull on my pants, socks, shoes, shirt, grab my wallet, keys, phone, cigarettes, weed, papers, and I go. I catch a cab. When I get home I open the letter.

Huck sleeps with me
And I sleep alone
You lie
You drink
That's all you do
You are not a writer

Rumi

# Chapter 2

The day after

"You're a liar," she said, then she kicked me out. Out of her life. Like I was nothing. Like I was dirt...

Today is the day after. And I want to kill myself. The cloud is black today. The cloud is not gray. Some days it's gray, some days even cream. On cream days I can be jovial. On cream days I can be a real laugh. My problem is those days are rare. See, *things* set me off. Small stuff pulls me down. Trivial shit shakes me. It shouldn't be that way, I know, but I have bad wiring...

I'd considered the words. I'd fucking considered them, then said them, then not heard them back, then got dumped. That's a lot of shit to deal with for a man with bad wiring. Meaning losing her devastates me. It leaves me thinking about the other thing. Again. About razor blades. And bathtubs.

You think I'm fucking around? Well, I'm not. It's in my DNA. My father, his brother, an uncle. It's in my fucking genes... This is biology. Not a cry for help... I hate those jerk-offs looking to get famous. Slicing sideways, parked outside the emergency room. Wrists held out, so the cameraman gets his angle. That noise is Hollywood. That's not me. I am not an actor. I am real. And I am sad. And my sadness is authentic... I'm seeing if things shift, if the cloud eases up. If not, then like I said... the other thing... And that's definitely real. The other thing is as real as it gets.

Not that I'll be missing much. If I go. The world is so full of shit, no one can breathe anyway... Have a look. A *good* look. See everyone running around, fake-smiling, plastic-laughing, praying the curtain won't slip? Just going through the motions. Dinner parties, promotions, drinks after work... vitamins on line, quality time. Billions of people, shuffled into boxes, medicating through the madness... Trying to find a fix.

If I *was* a writer, I'd write about that, about the fix.

If I was a writer.


Rewind three months

I'd stumbled into the diner where she worked. An all-hours joint, designed for people who kept strange feeding times. You know, eggs at four in the morning. One of *those* kinds of places. Drunk, as always, I'd been strong-armed through the doors by a good-time girl, a dayshift laborer at one of the handier gentleman's clubs, one of the seedier numbers. I'd been trying to get my end away, off the clock, free of charge, but she wouldn't let me at it. Not without pie first. And even though I was three sheets, and I never notice anything, I noticed her, the waitress, Rumi.

For days after, I'd come in and watch and get real mad. The way some of these assholes talked to her: get me this, change that, where's my coffee? swearing, no thank you, bad tip, no tip. Several times I wanted to follow her tables out into the lot, for a friendly word, introduce them to a hurting. And if God hadn't stricken me with such a crippling lack of ability, I would have. This one guy, a trucker probably, turned real nasty when she wouldn't give up her number. Called her a vagina. He called her the V word. I couldn't believe it. I'm a cunt but I've never called a girl the V word. The V word is off limits, and everybody knows it. Anyway, she just moved on to the next table, paid him no mind, like "fuck you, you can't hurt me." She had me after that. I almost called her over, told her she was amazing. But I didn't. That's not my style.

... My head held its usual tenderness. The mornings were getting steeper. I carried myself—everything throbbing—down sidewalks, past the downtrodden, the highflyers, crack houses, skyscrapers, bars, shops, street vendors. I walked clear across town, hoping that my lungs would fill themselves and push out the poison. Down a back alley I had to stop, throw up, spit, wipe my mouth. A sudden downpour of rain hit me. Karma working its usual. By the time I got to the diner, I was shriveled. I considered going back and changing but when I entered she was there, and smiling, and calling me over. She had never done that before: call me by my name. She. Knew. My. Name. Soon I had hot coffee, and a towel. She smiled at me. I smiled back, my chest thumping, hurting, thumping. "Listen," she said, "I've seen you, come in here, pretending not to watch me, and I admire your persistence and you seem like a nice guy—polite, tipper—so if you want to give it a shot, I can meet you outside at eleven, and you can buy me a drink, and tell me why I should go out on a proper date with you." She said it in one long breath. Then didn't wait for a reply. She just turned, and left.

... And you know the rest. I'd missed that date, lied about it, gotten a second chance, managed to fuck that up. Now here I was, the day after the letter, depressed, alone in my apartment, and thinking about the other thing.

Red (and Ed)

It got worse. After Rumi. I nosedived into the abyss. The hurt went into my bones and stayed there. I had never felt this before. This soul-crunching, heart-ripping madness. It ground me down, and sucked out my marrow.

For two weeks I was on autopilot. All I could do was go from bed to liquor store to couch to bed. I couldn't handle bars. I was too depressed for people...

There is an alleyway next to my apartment: a shortcut to the liquor store...

I met Red falling down the alleyway, drunk, tripping over bags of rolled-up essentials: of cans, old trousers, flat batteries. He had packed them for a war—for a battle with wind and rain and stealing. And I had spilled them with my legs, broke open his tied plastic bags with my clumsiness. You're in my house, his eyes said. Dead eyes that held my breath.

I was drunk, and he was drunk, and who was drunker I don't know, but I fumbled sorry (no eye contact and didn't mean it) just so I could be on my way, back to my apartment, bottles in hand.

But he stopped me... I got to my feet, checked the bottles for cracks. No cracks. I wanted to leave, needed to, but he stopped me. He put his hands out in front, saying stop, saying I had to, so I did.

It was noon, maybe a little before, and I'd had whiskey, and he'd had whiskey. And it came on me strong, hosed down on me, as he spoke: "You need to watch yourself," he said.

"Sorry," I said, intimidated. He was old and out of shape. And I was pretty sure he could take me.

With dirty fingernails sweeping the ground, he invited me to take a seat and spend time... And because I had nothing better to do, and my head was tired, and the way he said it was lonely, and I was too, and mainly, and above all, because he was tougher than me—that's what I did.

We got to talking over a bottle. We drank from it, me and him, passing it, back and forth, me and him, in a rhythm: talking and drinking, getting into it: him about the world, and what a cunt it was, me about Rumi, and how hard I missed her. And although listening was tough—I just wanted to talk, I didn't want to listen—connecting made me feel human. For the first time in a while.

And I didn't say it, but I was glad of the company. I had no other friends. And I was glad of the company.

... Red's company. Not Ed's company. Ed is Red's friend. He is skinny and black and about fifty and has wild hair and buck teeth. Ed is not my friend. Ed does not like me. I meet Ed a few hours after

I meet Red. He has a spot all the way over in the financial district, far away from here, where he says the begged money is okay—first thing in the morning, at lunchtime, and after five. By seven, he says, the place is dead, and he gets to run his spot. "No one bothers me up there. There's nothing worse than being bothered. And no one bothers me up there." He asks me my name, so I tell him, and he tells me I have a good name, a strong name, that he read *Tom Sawyer* when he was a kid, and that he liked Huckleberry more than Tom, and that I have a good name. I tell him thanks. He tells me not to take it personal, but, he says, I'm weak. He says he can tell I'm weak just by looking at me, and that he doesn't like weak people, and that he doesn't like me. I don't know what to say to that so I say nothing. I look at Red, but Red says nothing, so I say nothing. He tells me I look sad. I tell him I am sad. He asks me what I am sad about. I tell him about Rumi.

"I met a girl. She's a waitress. And a good girl. And I met her. And we dated for two months. Then she dumped me. She said that I was a liar. And that she couldn't be with a liar. So she dumped me." I show him the letter.

"A girl dumped you?"

"Yes."

"A girl you dated for two months?"

"Yes."

"Because she thinks you lied to her?"

"Yes."

"Did you lie to her?"

I don't say anything. I don't like how he's asking me what he's asking me.

"Did you lie to her?"

"Yes."

"What did you lie to her about?"

"That's not the point."

"Listen," he says, "you're weak." He turns to Red. "I'm going to go, Red. This kid isn't for me." I look at Red, and Red doesn't say anything, so I don't say anything either. Ed stands up. "Listen, kid, you got any money? I want a cheeseburger."

I reach into my pocket and pull out five dollars and give him five dollars.

"See here, why don't you give me ten?"

"I'm not giving you ten, Ed."

"Well, fuck you then."

I do not like Ed. And I am happy to see him go.

That night I sleep in the alleyway with Red. It is cold and dark and mean and bad. But it's colder and darker and meaner and badder in my apartment on my own. We drink whiskey all night. I pretend to listen. And when he stops talking—to take a swig of whiskey—I talk about Rumi. Until I take a swig. Then he starts up again. No one is listening. But we pretend to listen. It's just like real life. But at least I am not alone. The morning comes. And I am cold and I am wet and I can't take any more. Being homeless isn't like I thought. It is hard goddamn work. And I am not made for it.

"Listen, Red, I've got something to tell you, and you're going to think that I'm lying, then you're going to get angry, then you're going to want to hit me," I say, "but don't. Just listen." I'm still sore from a couple of rights—Red's one of those natural fighters—he hit me with last night: because I wouldn't give him the bottle, because he was finishing it too fast, and we were running out, and the liquor store was shut, and it had to last us until eleven, when I could buy more. I tried to reason with Red, about the drink, but Red's an alcoholic and you can reason with an alcoholic, just not about the drink.

"What is it, kid?"

"I'd like a promise first—that you're not going to hit me."

"Kid, I'm not going to lie to you. I could tell you that I'm not going to hit you, but we both know I've got no control over it. If it's any consolation, it's nothing personal."

I scurry back a little on my heels, to give me some distance, but he shuffles forward, keeping me in range.

"See this building, right here?"

"I'm not blind, kid."

"Well, I live in it. Apartment 606."

Red grins, then grins wide, then starts to shake, then starts to laugh. "You live in this building?" He slaps the concrete with his hand.

"Yes."

"And you slept out here?"

"Yes."

More laughing.

"And why would you do that?"

And I tell him. "Because I'm lonely, Red." And he stops laughing. And we don't say anything. Not for a while. We sit there in silence. I'm not good with silence, so I play a song in my head. I play Dinah Washington's "Me and My Gin." I only have one Dinah Washington CD, *The Best of Dinah Washington*, but I know all the songs on it, word-perfect. "Me and My Gin" is my favorite. Which is strange because I don't much like gin. But the song is great and her voice is great and it's a song I play a lot in my head. I like to play music in my head. Especially when I am alone, or nervous. Which is most of the time... I start to get dizzy. My stomach only has the whiskey in it and that doesn't feel too good and I throw up and my stomach hurts and I know I need to eat. There is a pizza joint a block over, next to the 7-Eleven, and it's a stand-up place. The pizza is good and cheap and by the slice and after closing, if they see homeless people milling around outside, they come out and give them free pizza. It's run by an Italian family, immigrants, and they are real stand-up. For some reason, though, they don't like me. When I go in, I get a look I don't like, like they don't like me, and that makes me nervous. So I hardly ever go. Maybe my head makes my world small. I don't know. All I know is I can't handle them staring at me today so I sit here with my stomach hurting. I drink more whiskey to make it feel good. But it feels worse... I decide that I want Red to move in with me. I know he'll be hard work but being alone is hard work and I'm lonely and I'm not doing too good on my own, so that's what I decide. I tell him. "We'll be on easy street, Red. No more sleeping rough. I have money, drink, everything. We'll be on easy street." I figure he'll be happy to be off the street, but instead he gets suspicious, and that upsets me.

"Shit, kid," he says. "I don't know you," he says. "How do I know you don't want to get me somewhere, do something, kill me or worse like something sexual?... Could be a serial killer, could be a sex-crazed, sick, stabbing, madhouse, crazy boy... what do you have to say to that, huh?"

"Nothing, Red. I don't have nothing to say to that."

"Well, work with me, kid, for Christ's sake, it's no good for me out here, I'm an old man."

He says *old* like he's saying *dying*, and I feel sorry for him. But I don't know what to do. I don't know what to do to convince him I'm not a sex-crazed, sick, stabbing, madhouse, crazy boy.

"How about you give me the key, let me check things out first *then* you come up five minutes later? Let's do that, okay, kid?"

That sounds like a good idea, and I didn't come up with it, and I wonder why I didn't come up with it. "Fine, old man." I hand him the key. He asks me the number again and I tell him "606" and he stands up, collects his things, and goes.

I wait the five, and another five, then go into the building, and head for the elevator. It's stationary, stuck on seven. I keep pressing the button but it won't budge. Someone has the porter key and has locked it off. *Fuck*. The tenants here rotate. A lot. This building is a game of musical chairs. I am in a game of musical chairs. And I hate it. There are always new faces appearing and smiling. New people to avoid. It is tiring.

While I wait for the elevator, I go to the mail slots, put my key in slot 606, jiggle it around— I have a bad key—and turn. Everything inside pours out like gravy, smothering me—flyers, bills, nothing handwritten. No love letters, or letters of any kind, just automated reminders, reminding me that no one cares, that I don't matter. I stick them back, cram them in as they laugh at me. "You don't exist," they say.

The elevator comes. When it opens a girl walks out. And not just a girl; she is someone I know, someone I used to talk to, a girl I had dinner with once…

I remember we drank a lot of wine. I remember that. And I remember her getting upset, but I don't remember why. It's been weird since then. Between me and her. Whenever she sees me, she puts her head down, and pretends *not* to see me. Like now.

"Hi," I say.

"Hi," she says. No eye contact. To stop her leaving, I block her way.

"Listen, about that night—"

"I don't have time, Huck. Got to run."

She puts her hands on me, and pushes, makes a little room, and squeezes past.

"Fuck you then."

Shit. I wish I hadn't said that. I'm always doing that. Acting hotheaded and regretting it right after. It's like a trait, like part of my makeup.

Elevator up to six...

I'm still feeling dizzy, struggling to walk, so I use the corridor walls to reach my door. When I get there I knock. I envision Red with the breadknife. I wonder if he would stab me. I mean *really* stab me. I think he probably would. But I need the company. I knock again. And again, and again, and again... Knocking, calling out, waiting, knocking, getting mad. The angrier I get, the louder I become. I get pretty loud. I give myself a headache. I put my ear to the door. All I can hear is the sound of the wood. Wood is pretty quiet. Red has the only key. Without

Red, *I* am homeless. I am homeless and Red has a home. The irony isn't lost on me. There is a spare key, but it's with a girl. A girl I dated a year ago. That relationship ended badly. Because of my temper. Now I am legally obligated to stay away from her. So her key is not an option.

My homosexual neighbor, the one I hate, opens his door, and mutters something. I can feel the anger rising. Muttering is for cowards. It is a violent form of cowardice. (I think about concepts, like cowardice, about what they mean. During my alone time, I work a lot of things out...) If he were smaller, and wasn't in shape, I'd have swung for him by now. *Look at him.* With his perfect teeth, all toned and tan. Check him out with his condescending helpfulness—always offering me this and that, and "we should catch up soon," every goddamn time he sees me. You can't catch up with someone you've *never* had a conversation with. I should say that too, right after I punch him in the face. He throws parties all the goddamn time, but has he ever invited me to one? No he hasn't. Not one, in all the time I've lived here. I didn't always hate him—his name is Chuck, by the way—I didn't always hate Chuck. I thought he was okay at first. But when he never invited me to his get-togethers, I figured him for a fake. I'm good at reading people...

"Everything okay there, Huckleberry?"

"Fine and dandy, everything's A-Okay, tip-top Chuck, see you soon."

I turn away and carry on banging. He closes the door, but no footsteps follow. I can feel him peering through his peephole. Eye-raping me hard.

The banging continues until Mrs. Lipton (I'll tell you about her in a minute) opens her door.

"My dogs are asleep, Huck, you know their schedule. If you've lost it I have copies."

"No need, Mrs. Lipton, I have it."

I am updated regularly about Lipton's dogs. About their kidney infections, upset stomachs, nap times. She writes it all in letters and posts them under my door. When I'm drunk, I read them. I like the way she writes. Sometimes I'll come home drunk, hoping to find one of her letters, slipped under my door, and if there isn't one I get bummed out, then settle for reading one of her old letters. I save them in a drawer.

"Sorry, Mrs. Lipton. My friend has the key. And he's inside, asleep probably. I can't get in."

"I can't have you banging, Huck. You know I like you, drunk that you are, but my dogs..."

I smile. She always brings up the drinking. But I like Mrs. Lipton, and I need her letters, so I let it slide.

"Sorry, Mrs. Lipton. I'll stop."

"They'll be awake in an hour—you can try banging then."

She waves, and goes back inside to her shows and knitting... Sometimes I think about Mrs. Lipton, on her own, and I get sad. She misses her husband. He's been dead twenty years. Sometimes we talk in the corridor. Even though I don't like making small talk, I do it. Hung over, drunk, or just not in the mood, it doesn't matter. I do it anyway. Because she is a good woman. And because there aren't many of those.

My back against the door, eyes closed, I drink, drink, drink until I drift.

# Chapter 3

Not a man

I get hit. I get hit hard. I scream out. I touch the back of my head. I brush it with my hand. No blood. I am lying in my doorway. I look up to see Red. He is smiling.

He is wearing my robe—a gift, although I don't remember from whom... I have never worn it. It is too beautiful. I would worry about ash, burns, spills... but he does not worry about these things, and he wears it. And without underwear. I say nothing. I can see ash on the robe—and grime and grease and spilt scotch.

"You crying?"

I ignore him. I recheck my head.

"It looks like you've been crying," he says. "Listen boy, enough of this crying bullshit. Crying doesn't get you anywhere. It just makes you to look wet and stupid and like a girl. You a girl, boy?"

"No, Red. I'm not."

I feel embarrassed. I mean, Red's been to war. He's been to Vietnam, for fuck's sake. What have I been to? Fucking psychologists is what. I tell Red that too. He says *that's* my problem. At a hundred and fifty an hour, it's taken the man out of me, he says. And I have to agree with him. Because Red's a proper man. And proper men, well, they could teach me a thing or two, you know, *really* sort my head out. I wonder about the army. Maybe I need to join up. Or the marines. I've always wanted to say I was in the marines. Or special forces. I bet even Red wasn't man enough for them. Getting in there, now that would be something. I make a note to check them out, have a look at their online brochure. Everyone's got an online brochure these days.

I put my hand out and motion for him to help me up. But he stares me down. So I use the door handle, which is hard because I'm still dizzy.

"Where've you been? I've been knocking."

"Inside." He yawns. My shirtsleeves ride up his wrists. I don't remember giving him my watch. "I took a nap," he says. He puts him arms back down. My watch disappears. He has scotch in his hand. A bottle.

"You found the scotch okay?"

He takes a swig, finishes the bottle and hands it to me.

"And my clothes?"

"Hey, fuck-nuts, *you're* the one who wanted me to come up to your apartment. Now you want to be a wiseass? Make cracks at my expense? Listen, if that's how it's going to be then I don't think—"

"You're right. I'm sorry."

I walk in and close the door. Red's things are steaming on my father's sideboard. That's the first thing I see, and it affects me pretty bad. The sideboard was my father's. He wanted me to have it, when he died. And then he went. So now it's mine. I don't have anything else of his—not a watch or a pen or a tie, or anything—except for a bunch of money (that threw me onto easy street, into oncoming traffic) and this sideboard, this woody shrine. And although it is ugly, and it sticks out, and it stares at me, I love it because it was his, because he wanted me to have it: because he loved me. I never put anything on it. Not when I'm in blackout, or feeling sorry for myself, or ever. Not *ever*. And now Red's things are pressing their mark, their decay, into its wood, and it kills me, overwhelms me with a sadness, a real deep blueness. I don't say anything though. He didn't know. He didn't know about my dad, about him dying or the significance of the sideboard. So I let it slide. Instead I just move his stuff off the top, and place it on the floor. Then I walk over to the couch. There's nowhere to sit. More of Red's things are smothered across it, flowing out of bags, stinking up the place. *It's smearing street grime all over cream fabric—at a million dollars a foot.* That's Mrs. Lipton's voice. It gets into my head a lot. More than I want. I block it out. It's a decent voice, but it's sad and mothering, and I block it out.

At the counter, I pour two glasses, big boulders, and bring them over. Then I go back and get the bottle. I sit down on my floor next to Red. We drain and fill. Drain and fill. Drain and fill.

I run a bath. Playing the host, and meaning it too, I give him first on the tub. I even offer fresh towels. I impress myself.

"Baths are for girls," he says. "I'm fine how I am."

I do not mention the smell. It hurts my nose and I do not mention it: tagging along, clinging, holding onto his clothes—my clothes, his skin—layers of it, climbing on top of layers, welding filth with filth, creating a monster. It is vile and wretched and rotten. And I do not mention it. Even though we are inside, and boxed in—and there is no outside to dilute its concentration; even though it jams itself into my eyes—I do not mention it. A man must have his dignity. Red must have his dignity.

"You crying again?"

"Sorry, Red."

"Jesus Christ, kid."

I do not say anything. I turn and enter the steam. I peel off my jeans and T-shirt, and brace myself. I am in. *Fuck.* All the water is sucked out of my body. The pain is relentless and heartless and all-consuming. I have entered hell, I am at its center. But I do not scream or squeal or cry. I do not want more abuse. More branding me a girl. Judging my backbone. I promise myself that I won't talk about Rumi anymore either. Red's getting tired of that, I can tell. He rolls his eyes whenever I bring her up—which is a lot, so he rolls his eyes a lot. I'm going to keep that sadness inside, keep that blackness bottled up, and add it to the rest, to that big pile of fuck-you. (It's getting bigger, too—the pile. It's getting out of hand...) I grab the bottle, tip it hard, swig, glug, force it down until the burning is outside and in, and equal. I close my eyes, exhale long and hard, and catch my breath. I take another drink, and keep my eyes closed, and more breathing, and another drink. I do not think of anything. Not the emptiness. Not nothing. I just close my eyes, and drink. Close my eyes, and drink.

That night we go to bed—filthy and drunk and huddled together—him snoring, both of us clutching bottles, CD player on. The Dead is playing... Have you ever listened to The Dead? I never have. Not until a few months ago. And then it was an accident. I bought the wrong CD. I got it from a shop. I'm no good at returning things to shops. So I kept it. The album is called *American Beauty*. It got me from the first track, a track called "Box of Rain." It is one of the most magical tracks I have ever heard. Now I listen to the CD all the time. I'm getting kind of bored with it now. I always do that, overplay the albums that I love until I ruin them. And I'm almost there, almost at that tipping point with *American Beauty*. I still love it, but I very nearly hate it... I lie here and listen to Red. He is passed out cold but he mumbles along. He knows all the words. I wonder if he's seen them, seen The Dead live, I wonder if he's a Dead Head. Me, I'd like to catch more shows. I always mean to, and I buy tickets sometimes, but crowds scare me, energy scares me, so I never go... I can't sleep. His smell makes my chest wheeze. It acts up my asthma and keeps me awake. I lie there, wondering how to get Red to like me. I've told him that I like him. I knew it was the wrong thing to do, even before I did it. I knew it was creepy. But I couldn't help myself. Most of the time, I don't have a good filter. And I've lost a lot of friends because of it. When I told him, he just gave me this look, like I was pathetic. Eventually, head spinning, I pass out...

"Huck!"

"What?"

It feels early and my head hurts and my body hurts.

"Wake up, boy, you ran out of scotch."

I rub my eyes, stretch, scratch my arms, my legs (I'm always itching), and let out a yawn. I always keep an emergency bottle, always. Just so

I'm safe—you know, for protection purposes. In a cupboard, behind some pots, it is well hidden.

"There's a bottle—"

"There *was* a bottle, behind some shit in a cupboard. I found it and I drank it."

I look at my wrist. No watch. "Hey, give me my watch back."

He ignores me.

"It's six in the morning."

"Okay."

"7-Eleven serves at eleven."

"Okay."

I try to go back to sleep, only he won't let me.

"Huck!"

"What?"

"What else is there to drink?"

"There's beer in the fridge."

"Anything else."

"No."

"Hard liquor?"

"No."

"I like hard liquor."

"That's cool."

"You have some? Because if—"

"No."

"Then what's cool?"

"That you like hard liquor."

"Listen, you little piss ant: when you were—"

"Red?"

"Yeah?"

"I'm really tired."

He ignores me.

"How about the neighbors?" he says. "They'll be awake soon, getting ready for work. They're probably already up. They'll have liquor. *Everybody* has liquor. Except the Moslems of course. And even most of *them* drink. So I wouldn't *not* ask them, just because of their religion. I think that would be racist—the not asking, I mean."

"Red?"

"Yeah?"

"I'm really tired."

"Will you at least try for me? I'd do it myself but my leg..."

I know about the leg. It was injured in the war. "And not just any war," says Red, "the Vietnam war, against those Vietcong sons of bitches." He spits on the floor after he says Vietcong. He has friends that died over there. Lots of friends. But he doesn't like to talk about it. But he talks about it a lot. For a man who doesn't like to talk about it, he sure does mention it, and more than now and again. I wish I'd have fought in the war. It must feel good to come back and be a hero. And I say that too. But Red tells me it wasn't like that. He says there was a lot of bad blood, a lot of bad blood when he came home. I feel sorry for Red. But I can't wake my neighbors up. And I say that too. But Red doesn't like hearing that. And he spits on the floor again.

"Can't or won't?" says Red, wiping the sides of his mouth with my shirt sleeves.

"Red, I'm really sorry but I don't know any of my neighbors. I've made a point of making sure I don't know any of them, apart from Mrs. Lipton, and she's a good Christian so I can't ask her. Besides," I say, "it's six in the morning. I can't ask a neighbor for liquor at six in the morning, Christian or not."

More floor-spitting.

"I don't appreciate your tone, son."

"Sorry, Red."

I feel shitty for saying no, especially because he's a war veteran. An old war veteran with a bum leg, and I just told him no. I don't feel good about that at all. I ask him if a case of beers will do him. I tell him I can manage that.

He thinks about that. For a while. He takes his time.

"Okay, Huck, make it happen."

I get out of bed, pad to the kitchen. The fridge kills me when I open it. The light jack-hammers into my eyes, and into my skull. Half blind, I grab the case, and stumble back into the bedroom.

"Here you go." I pass Red a beer.

Red guns the beer, and another, and a third. Then tells me he wants to watch a film.

I have a lot of movies. Over four hundred. Somewhere between four hundred and seven hundred. I've never counted them so I could be way off. There are a lot of them. I know that much. I have more movies than anyone I know. The only place you can find more is at a rental shop. I'm pretty proud of my collection. I need a big collection because for a while now my day has consisted of drinking, taking drugs, watching movies and being alone. Movies are great because they stabilize my moods. When I feel *this* way, I watch *that* movie. I know exactly what to watch and when.

Red rummages through my library until he finds something he likes. It takes a while. We watch *On the Waterfront*. I've had it for years. Had it filed away in my classics section, along with all my Newmans and Hepburns. I never watch any of them—"the classics"—I just own them because they're important to own. I tried to watch *On the Waterfront* once, but I ended up watching porn instead. I like porn. Way more than I like black and whites. They're hard to get into—black and whites, I mean, not porn. It's not cool to say that though, so people don't. Still, it doesn't mean it's not true.

So, here I am, trying to watch my favorite movie, for the first time. And I can't. Not properly. Every few minutes, Red has me checking my watch. He gave it me back. Eventually. And every few minutes he has me checking it. As you'd expect, I miss important plot points. See, that's another plus for porn: there's no story line. You don't get nuances that slide by you. It's always:

mechanic, teacher, repair guy, pizza boy. And the ending is always money... I ask Red to catch me up. He doesn't like that. He gets angry and tells me he's not my keeper. "Fend for yourself, kid," he says. "You got to learn to fend for yourself." Then he drinks the last two beers. Just guns them down like I don't exist. Oh boy, did *that* get the blood up. Yes sir. That's like stealing a man's fries. You just don't do it. I stand up for myself, though. I tell him it's not right what he did, that he'd better start treating me correctly, or else. "Or else what?" he says. "Or else," then I point to the door. He can tell I mean it too because he apologizes, and everything's cool after that. For about a minute—until he starts talking about Ed, *saying* he's a good guy, *saying* he needs a place to stay. "It's cold outside, Huck," he says. "You should let him stay with us." He looks around. "Plenty of room." But I tell him no, no way. I tell him I don't like Ed and Ed doesn't like me and there's no way he can stay. Red says that he's disappointed in me and I say that's okay and I say that he should drop it and, because he knows I'm serious now, he drops it. Yeah: living with Red is going to be hard goddamn work.

Dead on eleven, he's got me throwing on jeans and running out the door. *Hard goddamn work.* I look like I've just been caught banging the neighbor's wife. I'm pulling on clothes, zipper undone, shoes in hand, panting to the lift. I look guilty.

"Hurry Huck! I'm going to time you. One one thousand, two one thousand, three one thousand..."

I feel like a bum walking into the 7-Eleven. I always do. It's a block from my apartment. And they know me in there. They know I'm a drunk. They've smelled it on me in the morning. Loads of times. So now they look at me weird. Like, down at me. Especially the main guys: Asher and Tom. I don't mind Tom. He hit on a girl once, a girl I was with. I was at the back of the store, and she was at the register, and I heard the whole goddamn thing. Heard him trying it on. I did mention it to him. I didn't let it slide. And he said he was sorry, but not *too* sorry, he said, because she was *really* hot, and he had to try. And she *was* really hot so I didn't hold it against him. Tom is a good guy. A straight shooter. At the very least he's okay. But Asher. Fuck. Something about him just reeks of bad news. I can't put my finger on it, but there's something not right there. There's something very wrong.

Walking in is embarrassing. A lot of it has to do with the bell above the door, the alert that another deadbeat is here—buying gum, cigarettes, BEER, hotdogs, LIQUOR—cuts into me every time... Fridge first. Then counter. Without eye contact, I ask for four bottles of scotch. "Bag?" I don't look up. It's Asher's voice, calling me out, calling me a nobody. Of course, it *had* to be Asher, didn't it? I'm not surprised. This is how it always is, Murphy's Law following me around, going wherever I go, muddying my waters. Fucking Murphy and karma and Asher... *and* fucking Red: he's the one who pushed me out the door, the reason I'm here in the first place. Why do I let people order me around? If I don't reel it in, my kindness will do me over, mark my words... Anyway, Asher: without looking up, I can tell he's eyeballing me, just trying to start some shit. But I'm not playing. No fucking way. I'm not getting involved. That's what he *wants* me to do—but I'm not that stupid. Leaving the bag on the counter, I hand over some notes, grab the scotches, turn and leave. I leave the change, dollars too, on the counter, like I can't be bothered, like I'm *too* rich. The dollars restore the balance, telling him *you work for me*; telling him... *and watch your step, son*. As the door closes behind me, I hear: "Huck, you left your..." But I'm wise to it and, refusing to get drawn in, I keep on walking. But it's difficult to carry four bottles and a case of beer. And I drop one of the scotches. And it smashes on the sidewalk. It's far enough down the block that Asher won't have seen, so no harm done... Let me tell you about the 7-Eleven: it's a daily struggle, beating it. Every day it looks down at me and pisses on my lifestyle. I hate it. I tell myself that tomorrow I'll go to the liquor store four blocks down. It's a discount store. It only sells liquor. It has everything and it's all lined up and it's all on offer and there's no judgment and they give you trolleys so you can buy a lot. I'll take Red. We can worship together.


## Stocking up

We wake up naturally and at the same time—and within ten minutes we're out on the street, flagging down a cab to take us the four blocks. Four blocks is not four blocks. Not to an alcoholic. No, to us, four blocks is more like twenty-five or thirty. Throw in a bum leg and we're talking sixty to seventy blocks. Easy. There's no way Red can walk seventy blocks, and there's no way I can walk thirty, so we stand outside my apartment, arms flailing, until we find a compassionate driver who'll stop for us.

Our driver turns out to be one of the crazies. You know, one of those nut jobs you wish you didn't get, but are stuck with, so you just grin and bear it, and hope to make it out alive. And it's touch and go today because he keeps turning round to address us, as he steers with his knee, coin-tossing with our lives.

"See the problem, what you Americans..." he says, jabbing his finger at the air an inch from my face, "what most of you don't understand, is that it takes effort, it takes charisma..."

*Christ. Not today.* I am worse than normal today. The road is bumpy, and there's too much movement, and I'm not doing good. I'm close to throwing up. I wind my window down, just in case, then touch my forehead, mimicking an explosion with my fingers.

"Hey guy, I have a monster of a headache. And I don't mean to be rude but I just want to get to where I'm going. I don't want small talk, or to make friends or whatever. Please. Sorry. Thanks."

"Guy? What the fuck? Why you acting like we don't know each other? I sold you weed last time... You don't remember that? Are you fucking with me...?"

I am not fucking with him.

I've never seen this guy before. Guaranteed. I can feel myself getting angry. I hate these tricksters, always trying it on, trying to get a rise, or work an angle. I'm about to tell him that, too, about to tell him that I got his number, that I'm wise to it, when all of a sudden he sticks his head out the window, and starts going nuts on a cyclist. He terrifies this scrawny library-looking girl. First with the threat of grievous bodily harm. Then with a promise of forced sex. It's all very unnerving. I do not like this kind of confrontation and it shakes me up. I look at Red, but he's staring dead ahead, his face relaxed, like this is nothing. Like this is just a day at the beach. That reminds me: I need to check out the army, see how the sign-up works. The driver winds his head back in but his venom is still thick like yucca.

"Goddamn motherfucking deathtraps, endangering everyone," he yells. "I mean, shit—you can't hardly see them, then they're on you, you know? All that zigging and zagging..." He takes a couple of breaths. "You got to *breathe* from your diaphragm—really take it in *deep*, hold four, then out four. Do like ten of them, on four counts, got it?" I tell him I got it. "Good. Hey..." Then, oblivious to oncoming traffic, screeching tires, horns, my pleas for safety, he rummages around, desperate to find something. Over my protests, he patrols the ass cushioning underneath me, giving my cheeks a good going over—taking this ride from bad to worst. "Here it is," he says, "this is it right here..." He pulls out his phone and... he reads out my number. *Fuck*. "I tried calling you," he says, "you know, to see what was up, hang out, no big deal, but no one picked up, and I'm like 'whatever—I don't give a shit.'"

I hear Red chuckle.

We pull up at the destination.

"Here's fine," I say, thrusting ten dollars at him. I just want to get out, leave, be gone, but he's having none of it. He pushes my hand away.

"Your money's no good here."

So I give him twenty, cementing my generosity over his.

While the old timer groans and stretches and straightens his junk out, I make a note of the registration. I cannot do that again. So I take a mental plate shot.

If you're not an alcoholic, I don't know how to explain what it feels like walking in. Imagine there's something you care deeply about—but more than that, like you *need* it, and lust after it, and can't live without out it, and don't want to. And I tell you there's a store that has a limitless supply of it, and I can take you there, and it's all affordable. Imagine how happy you'd be... Well, walking in, that's how it feels.

I spot Jackie at the register. Good old Jackie. Reliable Jackie. She never judges. Not for morning visits, not when I'm shaking, not when I stumble, or fall in the aisles. She smiles and scans, and thanks me. And puts me on my way. Jackie makes me feel better about being an alcoholic. And for that I consider her a true friend... Today she sees me enter—cap low, shades on, Red by my side. We nod to each other. Jackie is apple pie. Me and Red get carts. One each. "Listen up," I say to him. Then I give him a layout of the shop floor—wines, beers, scotch, vodka, tequila... I tell him where everything is. And to get whatever he wants. Then we go our separate ways. I head straight for the tequila. That's the one I always forget, the one I always want, when I'm sat at home with bottles of everything but. Karma can do that. It can get psychological on you. I get my tequilas, and move over to the scotch aisle. There's an old man, tweed coat, patches on the arms. He gives me a disparaging look. Like a really bad look. Like I've done something horrendous. Like I shouldn't be in his aisle. Like scotch isn't for my kind, like it's not for people like me. Keeping eye contact, I reach into the trolley. I grab a bottle, open, and drink, and keep my eyes locked on his. He doesn't look away... he doesn't look away... then he looks away. Then he moves on. I should feel good, like I've won, but I don't feel anything. Not bad, not good, not anything. I just feel like he was here and now he's not. I keep filling my trolley, until I can't, until it's full. Then I look around for Red.

I see him in the far left corner, cozying up to a purple rinse in French wines. His hand gestures, his relaxed manner, the way he takes her card, caresses the hand, then kisses it—is all very Don Juan—*very* impressive. I'd not seen this side to him, so I hadn't considered Red as sexual. I'd figured the drink had drunk it out of him, dried up his lust, or stowed it away, left it somewhere waiting for a glimmer of sobriety to reawaken... But I'm wrong. Like I often am. (And more and more these days.) I watch Red, watch as he pummels the old girl—slapping her with the verbals, manhandling her with charisma. She's practically purring. He's doing a good job, a *great* job, and women eat that up. I watch him, see how he circles and closes. I take pointers, mental notes. I think about Rumi, about how much I miss her. I bet he wouldn't have fucked up with a girl. No. Red's a winner. Red's a goddamn superstar.

We get outside and hail a cab. I check the license plate. For ten bucks extra, the driver says, he'll help with our bottles. There are lots of bottles, and it's a good deal, and we shake on it. The driver wipes his hand. My palms are clammy. I need a drink.

There is twelve hundred dollars of booze in my apartment. We unpack it, and lay it all down in the middle of the room. We stare at it. I am happy, Red is happy. When an alcoholic takes ownership over this much alcohol, something magic happens. A feeling of safety washes over. The relentless tightness in the chest disappears. Everything becomes manageable. Everything becomes *okay*. We sit and drink and smile and stare at the stock.

# Chapter 4

My father

All men need a suit. That's what my father used to say. All men need a suit, a suitcase, a watch, and a haircut. *You have those, son,* he used to say, *you have those, you can look good and move and keep time doing it.* He was a good man, my father, and he said a lot of good things, and I miss him. I look at Red. He is dressed in my scrubs. He threw his rags away, traded them in for my scrubs. Now he sits there looking surgical. We spend the day, the night too, on the couch getting drunk, peeling off layers from the stack, getting messy, Red slurring Doors songs, me thinking about suits for him, about materials and cuts.

Barking wakes me, hammers at my head, smashes against my nerve endings. We'd been at it heavy last night, celebrating the windfall, and now I'm paying for it. Eyes still closed, I reach over Red, to the side table, grab a bottle, open and pour. The firewater beats up on my organs, sloshes against them, causing burn and damage, and a relief from the pain. Doctors will tell you to drink water. But they'll say a lot of things. Me, I don't trust them. They are too in the pocket of the pharmaceutical industry to be taken seriously. So I've given up water. It's the taste. I don't like the way water *tastes. And* the pointlessness of it, the way it just takes up space and has no purpose. Water just gets me mad. So a few weeks back I gave it up. Since then my head's been in a constant ache, and really sensitive to noise. So the barking gets to me. And wakes me up. *Lipton's dogs*. They churn out the noise, and bite at my eardrums, and I hate them. I've let it slide though. Lipton's like family. Still, it hurts when they bark. It makes me want to kill somebody.

I check the clock. It's late.

"Come on, Red," I say, "get up."

He doesn't move.

"I got a surprise for you."

He doesn't move.

He's awake, I know it. But he's old and stubborn and he doesn't move.

I keep on hassling him. Eventually he turns around.

"Leave me alone, kid," he says.

But I'm stubborn and I don't. And that earns me a bloody nose.

"Shit, kid, you okay?" he says when he sees the damage.

"Fine," I say, "but we got to go."

The blood must make him feel bad because, without me bothering him again, he gets up and dressed, and five minutes later we're out the door.

We stand in front of the building. Trying to flag a cab. It takes ten minutes before one will stop. We are in a good neighborhood, but we look homeless, and it takes ten minutes for a car to pull over. I give the driver the address, sit back, and close my eyes. I fall asleep. I never fall asleep in a car, but I'm so tired I pass out.

Next thing I know, Red's prodding me in the face with a dirty finger.

"Wake up, kid."

I want to throw up. He stinks, and I can smell it, and I want to throw up. I wish Red would take a shower. An old man has to have his dignity though, so I won't ever mention it—even though I can hardly breathe when I'm next to him, which is all the time.

"We're here," he says. "Wake up."

I tell him I need more time. I tell that to the driver too. "Just five more minutes, Mr. Driver." But the driver doesn't like hearing that. He gets angry. Then more angry. Finally he threatens me with bodily harm. So I get out. I pay him, cross the road, and stand outside the shop.

It's been a while since I've been here. Last time was with my father. My hand is on the door, but

I hesitate, I do not push, I just stand there. I pray they won't recognize me. I don't want them asking about my father. People always look at you a certain way when you tell them what happened. They have this pity about them that's hard to take. I doubt they will though—I look real different. I've changed a lot this past year. My skin is practically see-through and I've lost a lot of weight. No, they won't recognize me.

I push the door and the bell chimes. It is an expensive chime. It is not like the chime at the 7-Eleven. Eyes stare at us. Noses go up. We are not welcome here. Someone walks toward us. He is thin and angular and good-looking and bored. He is not smiling. He is not smiling. He is not smiling. Then he is right on top of us. Then he is smiling. He is one of the plastic people. He wants our money. He works on commission. He does not want to help. He works on commission.

"Excuse me, sir, can I help you?"

I point to Red.

"It's not for me, it's for him."

"What would he like, sir?"

He's still talking to me, and not Red, and that's not right, and I tell him so too.

"You should ask *him*."

He turns to Red, he smiles, he looks smug. I want to smash his face in. I am worried that Red will feel overwhelmed, unwelcome, that he will ask to leave, and I want to smash his face in. I am wrong. I am wrong about Red here like I was wrong about Red with women. He talks, and when he does his voice is loud, confident and clear.

"I want something light, son, no heavy fabrics, a fine cloth, forty-two long, double breasted."

The smugness fades. The angular man looks annoyed. He does an about-turn, and disappears. Red touches my shoulder. Puts his hand there, and leaves it there. And it feels good.

"You don't have to do this, you know. Not that I'm not grateful, but honestly Huck, jeans would be fine. Hell, there's nothing wrong with these scrubs."

"It's what you deserve, Red."

Red thanks me. He puts his arm around me and thanks me. And it feels good. I miss my father. And it feels good.

The angular man returns, eyes pumping anger. He wants money, but not *our* money. That's the impression I get, what his eyes tell me. Still, he brings six jackets with him. He puts them down, hands one to Red. It's a perfect fit. We buy the jacket, trousers, shirt, tie, shoes. The man at the counter recognizes me and offers his condolences. I pretend not to hear. He repeats himself, so I talk over him, until he takes the hint and stops talking. Red asks me what happened to my father. I tell him I don't want to talk about it. "Okay," says Red. He puts his hand on my shoulder and I feel like crying. I don't though. I just pay and grab the bags, and leave the store.

Next is a trip to the barber shop. Haircuts for the both of us. A hot shave for me, beard trim for Red. We get to the place, we walk in, we sit down, we wait our turn. The shop is a lively shop, a busy shop, and we sit and wait and watch and wait our turn. They do not look at Red like he's homeless here. He doesn't want to get his new gear dirty, so he's still wearing scrubs and he still looks homeless, but they do not look at Red like he's homeless here. Someone smiles at us, points to the seats—brown, leather, cracked, worn—and tells us to sit down. "There'll be a wait," he says, then he turns and goes back to work, cutting hair, telling jokes, cutting more hair, telling more jokes. This is an honest place, and I like it here, and I don't come here enough.

I sit in the barber chair, all bibbed up.

"What do you need?" says the barber-man.

"A trim," I say, "and a hot shave, please, thank you."

I always get a shave when I come here. They are great. They use hot towels. They make you feel new.

Red's hair is long and bad. They wash it three times before it gets cut. He asks for a trim, but then he changes his mind. He says he wants short hair. They do me quick, but Red takes a while.

But when they're done he looks great. He goes to the bathroom as I settle up, and when he comes out he's wearing his shirt and suit and shoes. He looks like a different person. But he is not. He is still Red. Only now he looks like he could buy a suit, and catch a cab, and be a productive member of society. I hate that. I hate that even though he fought for this country, risked his life for it, caused death and saw it, and did what he was told, it takes a suit and a haircut to earn him proper eye contact. That makes me fucking sick.

Next, we stop at a store to pick up a suitcase. He argues with me, tells me he has no need for it, but I tell him it's something that I want to buy him, and I'd consider it a favor if he'd let me. So he says okay.

Then we head to a shop that sells fine watches. Swiss watches. Swiss watches are the best. I have a Swiss watch. I want Red to have a Swiss watch too. I am not better than Red. I cannot give him my watch. My father gave that to me when I turned eighteen. So I cannot give it him. So I take him to a store to buy his own.

We walk in and Red goes up to the counter and asks for the cheapest watch they have. I tell him I'll be offended if he picks out the cheapest watch, that I want him to get something he likes. But he says he doesn't care if I'm offended, that he doesn't want a watch, and that I've already done so much for him, but that if I insist it has to be the cheapest watch. I tell him okay. The watch fits and Red asks how much and I tell the sales girl not to say and I go to the counter and give her my card and she runs up the watch and it's two thousand dollars. Two thousand dollars is the cheapest watch in this store. But good watches aren't cheap and I'm glad that I could buy it for him. When we leave the store Red wants to know how much the watch cost. But I tell him that's not his business, that we had a deal and I stuck to it, and that it wasn't very expensive. I lie to Red. But I only do it because he wouldn't have accepted it otherwise. Red's not like I thought he would be. And I don't think he would have accepted it.

With suitcase, watch, haircuts and suit, we head to a cigar bar in Old Town. It's a great place, a place I used to frequent regularly, back when I was the old me. The last time I was here I was on my own and drinking and chasing tail and someone died on the table next to me. He just keeled over. A few women screamed and the room went quiet and the ambulance men came and checked his pulse and wrapped him up and took him away. It was all very real. Afterward, everyone carried on drinking and smoking, like it never even happened. I had to leave. It really got to me that he died. I mean, he died *right* next to me.

We walk in. All I can think is: I hope Red likes it. I like it a lot and I hope Red does too. Everything is draped in purple silk, but it's tasteful, and not too much. The owner knows me. Or pretends to. He sees me coming, he smiles, he offers his hand, he snaps his fingers, he acts like I'm *somebody*. He acts. A waitress comes scurrying over, and leads us to a table in the corner. It is in the shadows, and the darkness acts like a two-way mirror. We sit, invisible, sipping slowly, looking like money. The thing with good tailoring is you get treated like you matter. Like now for instance, with the waitress; she is impressed, and bats her lashes; she pushes out her chest, duck-bills her lips. Right before I leave, she slips me her number, slides it into my palm, lets her fingernail linger. I'm reminded of the coked-up emaciation, with the emerald eyes. I make a mental note to phone her. The waitress tells me to call her sometime. She wants to use me, I know. She wants to ride my money wave. And that's okay. Life is about using and being used and being fine with both. Right and wrong are just propaganda concepts. They are system labels.

Back at the apartment, Red stands naked in the living room, eating gourmet chips, slugging coke. I offer him a drink and he says no and that's more for me and that's just fine. I ask Red why he's naked. He says because he doesn't want to mess up his suit.

I drink, keep drinking, and time passes. I look over at Red. He is passed out, genitals out. He looks peaceful. I wonder what his secret is, how he gets the calm. My chemistry says the answer is at the bottom of the bottle, not the ones from before, but the bottle in my hand. I drink more, I drain the bottle, I pass out.

When I wake up my head is banging and the clock says three and I'm covered in sweat and I feel real low. I am naked. I feel sick. I keep drinking, eating chips, hoping the feeling passes. I cry on the balcony. I listen to Dinah Washington. I fall asleep. I dream black thoughts. When I wake up it is lunchtime. The low feeling hasn't shifted. If anything, it is worse. I don't know what to do. I want to be saved. I don't know what to do... I get up, shower, cold jets, plenty of soap. I cover my skin in froth, I behave like a kid, I make a beard. I scrub and it hurts and I can't stop. I draw blood. I put on a nice suit, one I bought to take me to my happy place. But there is no happy place. I know that now. Only capped-teeth salesmen peddling rose-scented shit, selling gold-plated subterfuge. When I am dressed, I walk into the living room. Red has his suit on, and is back on the bourbon, and looks happy.

"Where are we eating? I haven't eaten Italian in years," he says. "Did you know I'm Italian, *I*-talian, did I tell you that? What I wouldn't do for homemade pasta, gravy, veal..."

I do not like Italian food. I used to. I used to love it but I had a bad experience—a bad first date, actually—and I haven't eaten it since. I'm like that: I hate things by association.

But Red is my friend.

"I know a great place," I say. "Best veal chop in the city."

## I-talian food

A quiet African American, with rosary beads, and a Bible up front. He doesn't say a word. I tell him the address, he smiles, nods, checks his mirrors, and drives off. He doesn't have questions, or opinions he needs to share. Like Jackie, he is apple pie. When I get out, I give him ten extra. He says it's too much. I give him twenty.

We have a good table. I'd phoned ahead, used a fake name, someone famous, a Chicago actor. I told them I needed good seats, nothing near the toilets, out of the way, but not *too* out of the way. I told them I wanted to be seen but not to be seen wanting to be seen. I love fucking with people. I get off on it. As we are shown to our seats, I pass the girl from my apartment block. She is on a date. By how animated she is, I can tell it's a first or second: an early date. Either that, or he has money. I know that sounds bitter, but that's how the world works—how women work the world, as the world works them. When she sees me, she stops smiling, and looks away. We sit, we order Martinis, we eat the olives, we wave at the waiter. He ignores us at first, pretends not to see us, but we keep waving until he comes over.

"Listen, the wine: get me something smoky, and pokey and not oaky, okay?"

The waiter is good: he doesn't smile, just nods small, and disappears. The girl leaves with her date. He is older than her. She is mid-twenties, he early forties, and out of shape. It's a money date.

The wine comes, gets drained, so we order more, another two bottles. Red orders the veal chop. I order the veal chop. I don't want veal. I want sea bass. But if his veal looks better than my bass, my meal will be ruined. The food comes and goes, same with the wine. The check comes. I'll never drink wine again, not as long as I live, never again. Red sees the bill, and curses out loud. The ride home is quiet…

Back at the apartment, I take off my suit, and sit on the balcony, and stare at the brick wall that is my view. I should have bought a front-facing apartment, something that looked out onto the street. I don't know why I didn't. I think I was in a rush to buy. I wanted to own, to be an owner, so I took the first thing they showed me. It's a cool building though, a new-build with high ceilings, so it's not all bad. Still, the view sucks. I feel like a sucker whenever I look at the bricks.

I count them, top left first, going right, then down. I am still angry about the check. It's not the money. I can afford the wine. It's being taken for a ride that burns me. I feel my father looking down at me, looking down on me, when that happens. And I don't like it.

I smoke a joint, and think about my father, about my view, and about the value of a dollar. Red comes out, sees me, and sits down. He is naked and next to me and our thighs are touching. I carry on smoking. Red clears his throat.

"I haven't smoked a joint in a long time," he says. "I've always been more of a drinker. Plus that shit's expensive. Say, how expensive *is* that shit?"

So I tell him and he whistles. Red has a good whistle. It's long and piercing, and what with me giving up water, it hurts my ears, and I have to ask him to stop. He stops and asks if he can smoke with me. I tell him sure. I do not warn him that the weed is strong. In my experience that information is best learned for oneself. He takes the joint out of my hand, and we sit there and smoke, and we don't talk for a while, and we just get high. And it's good having company.

And suddenly, and out of nowhere, someone says something and we're laughing so hard that my sides hurt. And I don't know what was said but I'm wheezing and crying and gasping for air. It feels great to laugh from the belly. And I forget about my father, the view, and the bad check. And I just get high and laugh.

And then it gets quiet. And no one says anything. Because weed can do that to you. You can be laughing one minute, zoned out the next, paranoid sometimes, sometimes social. And no one says anything. Until Red turns to me.

"Mind if I ask you something?"

I stay quiet.

"It's kind of personal."

He puts his hand on my shoulder.

"Okay," I say.

"What happened to your father?"

I put my hand over his, and push it off.

"I don't want to talk about it."

"Sorry," he says.

"It's okay."

"I shouldn't have asked."

"It's fine."

It goes quiet again. Time passes, but slowly now because it's awkward. Red talks first. He's not a big talker, I mean, he talks, but he doesn't "talk"—not about personal stuff. So it's weird hearing him open up. I don't know if he's doing it so I'll tell him about my father, or because we're building trust, or because he's high. And it doesn't really matter. I listen anyway.

He tells me he has a son. That he's never seen. That he might have grandkids. *Might.* He doesn't know, he says. "I don't dare find out," he says, "or deserve to try... Jesus, Huck..." He cries. Red says crying is for pussies. But that can't be true. I am watching Red cry, and Red is no pussy. So that can't be right. I sit very still, because I don't know what to do. I tell Red I want to help find his son. Red doesn't like hearing that, he thinks that's a bad idea. I tell him that he might be right. That it might be a bad idea. But that it might be a good idea. And that there's no harm in trying. I ask him what he has to lose. Red doesn't say anything back. And for a long time we sit and say nothing. When Red turns to me, he asks me not to look for his son, and not to mention it again. I tell him okay. He makes me promise. I tell him I promise. He asks me if there's anything I can tell him about my father, since now he's told me about his son. I think for a while.

"I'll say this, but then that'll be it. Okay?"

"Okay."

"You have to promise me, Red. Promise me that you'll drop it."

"I promise, kid."

I make him swear on his son. He doesn't like that, but I press him so he does.

"My father gave up after my mother gave up. It runs in the family. And that's all I'm going to say."

"Okay, kid."

"So drop it."

"Okay, kid. I'll drop it. I won't mention it again."

And then I pass out. I am stoned and drained, I am tired and I pass out.

Red shakes me awake. I feel groggy, and I want to go back to sleep. I ask him what he wants. He says he has something important to tell me. "I like you, kid," he says, "and I needed you to know that." Then he hugs me, so I hug him back. He says that we need to stop talking about sad shit. "Everyone's got their sad shit," he says. "The trick is not to think about it." I tell him okay. Going to a shrink at $150 an hour—and talking about it—has never made me feel better. It's always made me feel worse, the remembering. That's probably why I drink, to forget. So I tell him okay. "Go back to sleep," he says. He closes his eyes, and I close mine, and I go back to sleep. And I dream about my father. The good stuff. Just the good stuff.

Jimmy the Jew: medicine man

When I wake up I go to roll a joint, but there's hardly anything left. Only a little, not enough for a joint. So I put it in a pipe and smoke it, and get dressed and leave. Red is snoring on the couch. So I make a quiet exit.

I take a cab to see Jimmy the Jew...

I hate these trips, they make me sweat. It'd be a lot easier on my nerves if he delivered. I told him that too. I said I'd pay extra, but he said no. I said I'd buy in bulk, but again he said no. So I threatened to go elsewhere. He said fine. "Go elsewhere," he said. I was bluffing of course. And I would have told him that too, I would have told him that I wasn't serious, that I was just joking, but he stopped picking up my calls, so I couldn't. I went a week without weed and it was terrifying. In the end I paid a two-hundred-dollar "apology fee," and he let me back in. I was happy to pay it. Jimmy has the best weed in town. Anywhere else is second best, and I was happy to pay it. Jimmy is my medicine man.

The ride over is nervy. I get like this when I run out of weed. The same thing happens when I run out of booze—just not as bad, because everywhere sells booze. Not like weed, where there's only Jimmy. I worry about Jimmy dying. I worry about that all the time, so whenever I see him I buy big. Just in case.

Because of the margins, there are lots of dealers. But good dealers—reliable dealers, dealers who have great product, and don't rip you off—are hard to find. That's why Jimmy the Jew has a lot of customers. And why sometimes he runs out. He keeps an emergency stash, for his preferred clients. But I'm not in that circle. Not yet. I want to be, and I've mentioned that to Jimmy, but he tells me these things take time, that I need to be patient. I've learned my lesson with Jimmy—I've learned that he runs the show—so I tell him okay.

The cab pulls up. I get out. I enter the building, and sign in at the desk. I use a false name, a Disney character. I go up to the seventeenth floor. I like this place. It's like a hotel. I knock on the door... Two inches, a set of eyes, chain off, he pulls me in. I am anxious. That's how I get around Jimmy. He is intense. He lifts a lot of weights, drinks a lot of protein shakes. He smokes a lot of weed. He doesn't like to leave his apartment. He is paranoid that people are out to rob him. Which is fair enough. His place was robbed recently. Jimmy's sure it's someone he knows.

"What's up, young 'un?"

A detailed handshake.

"Everything is everything, baby."

Jimmy is a Jew from Highland Park, family money, private schools. But he pretends that he's black.

"Come in, come in, you want grape or red?"

Jimmy drinks a lot of Kool-Aid. His teeth are in bad shape.

"No thanks, brother, I'm in a rush today." I look at my watch. "So I can't stay."

"Sheeeeet nigga, sit your ass down, and let's smoke a joint. We never hang out me and you."

This is not true. Jimmy always makes me sit and smoke and act like a gangster for at least two joints before he lets me leave. He relies on his clients for company. I feel sorry for him.

I tell him no problem, sit down, roll a joint out of his weed...

I am high and Jimmy is high. And in a minute it will come. I know because it always does.

"Listen Huckleberry—I've got something I've been meaning to ask you. The thing is, I can't work out who broke into my apartment. I mean, I've thought about it, I've thought about it *a lot*, but I'm having trouble working it out. What've you got to say about that?"

"I don't have anything to say about that, Jimmy. I guess it's the state of the world... it's a fucked-up place. You can't trust anyone."

Jimmy nods, and stares, and his muscles move.

"You're right... everyone's a snake."

"Right."

"But who was it, you think?"

I feel unwell.

"What's the matter, Huckleberry? You look edgy."

"I'm fine."

"So who took my stuff?"

"I don't know, Jimmy. Honest I don't."

"So that's how you're going to play it?"

"It's the truth."

"Swear on the Bible?"

"I swear on the Bible."

"I didn't know you were a Christian, Huck."

"I'm not."

"So why the fuck are you swearing on the Bible?"

"I don't know, Jimmy. I'm high... Sorry."

Jimmy goes into the bedroom, and reemerges with his red book. He sits next to me. Our thighs are touching.

"One Sony Television—50 inch; one blender—can't remember the make; one set of Aviano speakers—a present, irreplaceable; one amplifier—Onkyo design; two seasonal effective disorder lamps—make unknown, but expensive; twenty pounds of weed—twenty *fucking* pounds of high grade weed—*very* expensive; one watch—Omega..."

It goes on like that for two pages. When he's done, he closes the book, breathes heavy, and turns to me.

"You got anything to say?"

I tell him no.

"Okay," he says. "Listen—it's not that I don't trust you. But I had to ask. I'm asking everybody."

This is the eighth time we've had this conversation.

"I understand, Jimmy. No problem. I have to go though, so..."

"Bullshit. We never hang out. *Die Hard* is about to start."

Jimmy refuses to sell me weed until I've watched *Die Hard* with him. He knows the script, all the dialogue, word for word. He mutes the screen, and does all the parts, accents too. It is impressive and painful and time is slow... The end credits roll.

"Pretty good, huh?

"Yeah."

"You name me one other dude who can do that."

"I can't, Jimmy. Very impressive."

"Exactly. Pretty fucking tight... Okay, kiddo." He gets up. "I've got shit to do and I can't have you hanging around here all day. So what do you want?"

"Two ounces is good."

He goes into the kitchen and opens a cupboard. He takes out bags, and scales, and weighs me out two ounces. "Money." I give him the money. I tell him I'll see him soon. He lunges in and hugs me. I don't know what to do, so I hug him back. Then I leave...

Outside his apartment, I wait for a cab. As usual, I stand at the corner, paranoid, certain that arrest is imminent. The problem with Jimmy's weed is it's *too* damn good. Even in ziplock bags, you can smell it from a block away.

As I wait for a cab, I witness something bad. A cyclist cuts in between traffic, gets hit and goes flying. He lies in the middle of the road; people are screaming, people are staring, people are walking by. His limbs are bent unnaturally. He does not move. I cannot see his eyes, but I imagine the glaze, the draining out, life leaving. I go cold. I see a cab, I wave it over, I get in, I leave. I tell myself that the cyclist was in a movie, that it wasn't real, that he'll be fine.

*I walk up the stairs. The stairs that creek, have always creaked. This is my childhood home. The only home I know. I call out. But nothing comes back. I check the bedroom, the one my mother left, packed her stuff and walked away from three years ago, just vanished, no note... And nothing. It is empty. All the rooms are empty... The bathroom is locked. I knock. I call out. And nothing. I know he is behind the door. I keep calling out, keep calling out. And nothing. I don't know what to do. I try the handle. The door is locked. I keep calling out and knocking and trying the handle. I feel useless. I don't know what to do... I am not too worried. My brain says that he'll be okay. That, yes, he's been sad since my mother left, but he just needs time, and me, and he'll be okay... Then I get worried. Because I know he's behind the door. And not answering. And that's not like him. Worrying me like that... "I'm going to break the door down, Pop. I'm worried about you, Pop. And if you don't say something, I'm going to break the door down." He doesn't answer... And I know before I see. But I don't believe. I need to see it, see it with my own eyes. And I break the door down. It is an old door and I break it down with a run and a kick and the door breaks down and the door breaks down and the door breaks down and... the door is broken. And... no no no no no no no no no no no. My beautiful Pop. The water is red. No no no no no no no no...*

The aggressive sadness becomes too much and snaps me awake. It is the middle of the night. It is a nightmare night. And it feels like I'm there all over again. In the bathroom all over again. With the sad red water... He was my best friend. My very best. My only friend. And he left me. And now I am alone.

I grab my keys. I take a cab. I go to see Milly.

# Chapter 5

Rewind: The day after I buried my father

I have no one

Yesterday I saw him, lifeless and buried
there was only me, no one else
he stopped talking to people after she left, cut them out
and no one knew, and no one came
she didn't come, my mother, she didn't come
she probably didn't know, but still, she wasn't there
... and she was never there
I only had him, and he took that away, stole it from me. And now
I have no one...

I walk the streets, aimless, numb
I walk into bars, sit down, order nothing—just sit, exist, order nothing, get asked to leave
so I leave
and I walk, into another bar
and another, and another...

A girl starts talking to me
I don't know when, what bar, what time, why
but she starts talking to me
and I don't know how or why or when
but we go to her place, we sit and we talk
and I tell her
stuff
I remember that
I remember talking to her
telling her about my father
the suicide, the red water, finding him
I tell her about the loneliness
about how much I miss him
I cry
I tell her about the funeral
about it being only me
about him being my only friend...

And she talked to me
I remember that
I remember her talking to me
telling me about her pain
lots of pain, she had lots of pain

Two strangers
all night
sitting up talking
sharing, connecting, crying, drugs, drinking,
connecting, crying
and it was all too much

and it was just enough
and it got me through
and Milly got me through

... and he was my only friend
and now I have no one.


## Milly

Sometimes, when the cloud is black I visit Milly. Sometimes, I'm in such a bad way I just can't. So I sit in the bathtub, and think about joining my father. Sometimes it'll be months between visits. Sometimes days. But each time it's the same. I show up unannounced, high and drunk, and in a bad way—and she never judges. Sometimes we talk, sometimes we have sex, sometimes we do neither, just sit there in silence. But I see her, that's the thing. *I see her. And she sees me.* And that's how it is, between me and her.

Milly is a prostitute. She told me that the first night, when we were talking. We were at her place when she turned to me, put her hand on my shoulder. "Listen, Huck, I have to tell you something. And you won't like it. And you may not want to see me again. But I have to tell you. Because that's how it has to be between us. We have to tell each other the truth. The thing is..." She hesitated. "I'm a prostitute." I told her okay. That I didn't care. I asked her if she wanted money. I told her I had money, and she could have it, and how much. "I'll never take money from you, Huck. Not ever." And she never has. And that's just how it is, between me and her.

Cab over is a bitch. My chest is shitty, like I'm not quite, but on the way to, coming down with something rotten. The driver keeps looking in his rearview. Every time I cough he looks at me like I'm pissing against his backseat. I've done that, you know, with the seat, but only once, and I was very drunk... The driver is a talker. I hate talkers. He gives me the skinny on life, the Cubs, the Bears, women. It is a long ride... When we get to Milly's I give him the fare, the exact amount, no tip. If you're thinking: what about his kids, sister in Mumbai, rent, broken toilet, no gas, electric off—well, maybe you're right, and maybe I'm an asshole; but I hate talkers, so I paid him to the penny, and not a red cent over.

Outside her block, I buzz, and buzz, and keep buzzing, until she answers. I tell her it's me.

"Fuck," she says, but not in a bad way—she's just surprised. "I'm with a client. Can you wait until I buzz you in? Sorry, Huck."

Whenever I turn up I have to wait. Milly is a popular girl. She is pretty and young and does whatever you want.

"Sure," I say, "that's fine. I don't care."

... That's Buddhist, you know: the not caring. I was on a toilet once and I read an article about it. It was at a friend's house—an artsy friend, a right book reader—and I was doing coke and I had the shits and I was in his bathroom, and that's when I read the article. It was a great article. I took the magazine home with me. I stuffed it down my pants and smuggled it out. Anyway, I read the article a lot before I lost it, or someone stole it, or I misplaced it. It said that people who don't care are "seekers." Which makes me think that maybe I'm one too. Only, I drink and fuck and take drugs and am constantly on a suicide ledge, march, watch (depending on the day, hour, conversation), so I don't think I'd pass their special tests. People are always doing that: setting you exams, examining you. Just so they can weed you out. So they can tell you that you're no good. I fucking *hate* people. I don't think I'm a Buddhist, or if I am, I'm not a very good one.

... I call it *the fury*. Only it hasn't happened for a while, and never around Milly. I feel the anger rising, as I sit and wait and imagine upstairs. I am white-hot and raging. Some low life is making her do things. For dirty money. And it kills me. And I could kill... I'd offered to take care of her, get her out of the game, but she said there couldn't be money between us, that it would ruin things. I still don't get that. I'm offering her a way out, no strings, and she doesn't want it. And the anger is rising.

I sit on the steps outside her block. I sit and smoke and think about what he's doing to her, what he's doing to my Milly, what she's letting him do. *Murder.* I think about murder. The word does not scare me. I am thirsty for it.

The door opens, and out he comes. I look away, I look back, I stand up, I put my hand out, meaning stop. He looks frightened. He looks like I want him to look.

"What do you want?" he says.

I step forward. I am in his face. My heart is racing. I am nervous, I am scared. But the fury buries it. And I can hear my voice.

"You had a good time up there, did you? A good time at my expense, when you knew—*knew*—I was sitting on the fucking doorstep, waiting... like a fucking cunt. That means you think I'm a cunt. You think I'm a cunt? I think you're a cunt."

I spit when I'm worked up. His face is covered.

"Look buddy, I don't know—"

I step back, and swing. I use my hips for power—lessons from the cab driver kicking—but somehow I miss... Some people are soft and cuddly and reasonable and kind, but if you threaten them, well, then this other *thing* comes out of them. It's not really who they are that comes out, it's not the *real* them—the real them is soft, cuddly, reasonable, kind—what comes out is their desire for survival... When he fights me, when this man fights me, he fights like that, like he will do anything to survive, like an animal backed into a corner. His eyes bulge, he shrieks, he lashes out—balls, eyes, nothing is off-limits... Me, I do not fight like that. And I am beaten and beaten bad and hurting and on the floor and bleeding. Wishing I had a gun. He crouches down, puts his mouth to my ear.

"Don't show your face around here again."

"Fuck you, asshole."

I get more kicks—to the face, balls, ribs, stomach, throat. The throat hurts the worst, worse than the balls... In my time, I've taken a lot of beatings—restored a lot of manhood—but today is a real going over, I mean a *real* going over; I need medical attention... Right now, I should be in a hospital bed, nurses hovering over me, fussing. I should be on a morphine drip. Covered in expensive bandages. But I don't have insurance. All my money, and I am uninsured. *Fuck*. No insurance card means they park you in the waiting room, then just leave you there to die... No. No, I'm better off out here...

He walks away. I lie here. I feel like I am dead... I hear muffled talk—behind hands, private chatter. Like they're making a plan, and keeping me out of it. *Footsteps*. They are closing in on me. I try to lift my head, just a little, but I get dizzy, so I stop. I lie back down. I wait. I wonder if they will rob me, stab me, hurt me, fuck me. This is not a good place for beaten people. Milly has cheap rent. Two voices—back and forth, back and forth.

"Hey...? I don't think he's breathing. Fuck, should we call an ambulance? What do we do? Is he bleeding? He looks like he's bleeding. What time is the party? Christ, why am I even thinking about that? I am such a shit. Fuck. Oh fuck..."

"You need to calm down. Here..."

"'Get that away from me, listen..."

"Fine. More for me... Look, he'll be cool. I've seen this happen all the time—he probably just fell over, or something, probably just another drunk homeless guy without insurance. You know they won't see him without insurance. He's better off here. And we're going to be late... Fuck, we *are* late, come on."

"We're not just going to just *leave him*, for Christ's sake. He looks hurt. You can be a real asshole sometimes..."

It's a gay couple. I can tell by the tone of their voices. I breathe a sigh of relief. Gays are less likely to rob you than any other demographic. It's their feminine nature. I read that in a magazine. I like magazines. I like gay people, too. I tried to kiss a guy once, but when it came down to it, I buckled.

One of them gets closer. I can smell perfume: roses, cinnamon, grapes... It strikes me that I have a great nose. I know that shouldn't be on my mind, all things considered, but it's one of my best qualities, my sense of smell; plus you can't help where your head takes you. I wonder what kind of job that could get me. Probably something high up in the drinks trade, something in wines or whiskies, or brandies perhaps. Not that I need a job, but if I did, it's nice to know there's something I could excel at, somewhere I could make a name for myself.

Someone touches my neck.

"He's breathing. Thank fuck for that. Hey…? Hey fella…? You okay?"

I can smell toe now. I try again to get up, this time using my elbow. Slowly, I lift my head.

"I'm fine," I say.

My lip has grown. It drips onto my fingers.

"You don't look fine."

"You smell of roses and cinnamon and grapes."

"Excuse me?"

"The scent, the perfume, what is it?"

"It's erm…"

I can't make out what he says.

"Never heard of it."

"Yeah, well, Winston Churchill used to use it."

"Used to? What happened?"

Now the other one talks.

"Listen. Do you want us to get you an ambulance?"

"I'm fine, I fell, I fall a lot. I'm a drunk."

I put my hand out, motioning for help. They get me to my feet.

"Thanks."

I put my arms around them. I pull them in tight, hug, squeeze. One of them hugs back. Briefly. They go. I am alone.

The blood is all over my face. I wipe it, but it comes back—thick and slimy and smelling of metal. There are holes, I am leaving me, I am pouring out. I buzz, she answers, she lets me in. I open the door, start climbing the stairs. She is on six. The building is old, there is no lift, I am on fire by three. I have to stop. I have to wait for my lungs to stop exploding, for air to enter, poison to leave. I see faces, dead men, ghosts on these stairs. And they scare me and I push on. I climb the last few flights, and the sadness grows. She used to talk of leaving, of a finish line, an end date, but not anymore. Now there is no hope. Now there are only vacant eyes, glassed over, waiting. There are physical changes too. She still looks young, but her face has turned toxic and bloated and looks out of place on her stick-thin frame. Recently she has gone from smoking heroin to injecting. She is sliding, it's coming for her. And there's nothing I can do. At the outside she has ten years. And that kills me. And there's nothing I can do.

I reach her apartment, the door is open, I go in. The walls are stained and the floor is stained and the air is stained. I go into the kitchen. She isn't there. She hears me and calls out. "In the bedroom." I walk in, I see her on the floor, stretched out, eyes closed. She doesn't like the bed. The bed is for money, she sleeps on the floor, when we have sex we have sex on the floor. "Milly." She opens her eyes and sees me: beaten, half-dead, swollen, bloody. She doesn't say anything. I am always in bad shape when I come around, always in need of a fix. "You okay?" I tell her I'm fine, that I asked for it, that it doesn't hurt, that it's no big deal. She tells me to go get the vodka, and I do, and we sit on the bed, and we drink and get drunk and she plays with my feet. She has a thing for feet. She says I have beautiful long finger-toes. She likes to paint them. When she's high she messes it up, and has to start over, and it can take a long time, but painting my toes makes her happy, so I let her. Today we don't have sex. And we don't talk. Today she does heroin and she paints my toes and she asks me to hold her and I do and we fall asleep on the floor. I wake up and I let her sleep and I go downstairs and I catch a cab. This is a bad neighborhood and there aren't many cabs so it takes a while.

# Chapter 6

California calling

Driving home, I see a basketball game and it looks good. I want to watch it, and stop thinking about Milly, so I tell the driver to pull over. He doesn't like that.

"This is a dangerous neighborhood," he says. "It's a bad idea." And he doesn't pull over, just he keeps on driving.

"Here." I hand him twenty dollars. "Pull over."

The money talks, stops the car. A quick turn of the wheel and thirty seconds later we're parked on the street overlooking the game.

I slink down in my seat, keeping myself out of view, and watch. I watch the players, big ones, small ones, fat ones, tall ones, all sizes, all vying for the ball. No one passes. Basketball is not a team sport. Everyone out here is a superstar and basketball is not a team sport. The game is rough, competitive, foul-mad, but nothing gets called. There are no fouls in basketball... Then something happens. A kid gets hit. A skinny kid, one of the younger ones, maybe ten. An elbow catches him in the nose and he collapses, and he holds his nose, and half his face is blood. Then two people are fighting, then four, then more, then everyone, and all hell breaks loose... My heart shifts into overdrive. From the safety of the car I feel in danger. My heart starts to thunder. The man looks at me.

"I think we should leave."

He waits for the nod, I give him the nod, he pulls out from the curb, we leave. We ride home in silence. The radio is on and playing Eric Clapton and I feel like such a girl, having a heart that races...

My phone rings. It is California. I do not answer it. I think about Milly. I get sad.


The Lipton lie

I enter the building and press for the elevator. I consider opening the mailbox but decide against it. I am scared that I won't be able to cram it all back in. Right now, from the outside, it looks like the rest. It is normal: it makes me look normal. The elevator opens and out walks Lipton. The way she stares at me, the sadness, reminds me that I'm getting careless. She has my father's eyes. She looks down, focusing on my hands. They are empty today. Normally I have carrier bags, boxes. Normally I am clutching medicine. I like Lipton, but she's always catching me reloading, always finding me clinking along the corridor, trying to blend into the walls, using them to hold me up. I'm pretty sure she watches her shows on low so she can hear me coming, so she can open her door, and give me the look.

"Hello, Huckleberry.'

"Mrs. Lipton."

I am nervous. She's blocking the door. I want to go but she won't let me. I don't know what to say.

"How're the dogs?"

"Dogs are fine, feeding again, which is a blessing." She kisses her rosary. I think about church. About being a better person. But then quickly dismiss it. It takes hard work: doing the right thing, the Christian thing. It drains the life out of you. It'd probably do me in. You can tell the do-gooders by their early aging: thirty-year-olds looking forty, fifty-year-olds looking seventy. Lipton is looking old, older than before, and before she looked old. Lipton is looking a couple years over the finish line. I'd be dead if I was a religious man, if I were as Christian as her.

"You okay? You look a little peaked."

The truth is, I'm not feeling too good. I rarely am these days, especially these last months. I'm getting symptoms, signs, and ignoring them. I won't go to a doctor, because, well, I've already told you why, so I have to sit with it. Not that I'm in denial; I know what it all means. Still, I can't let the old girl know. It'd be the death of her. The Samaritan noose is closing in on Lipton, tightening around her good-hearted neck. I can see it coming any day now. What will happen to her dogs? Will they become mine? Will I have a choice? What will I do without her letters?

"Huckleberry?"

"What?... Oh, yeah, I'm fine. I just need to lie down."

"Listen. You need to stop drinking."

"I know Mrs. Lipton, you're right. I need to cut down. It's just been a little heavier that normal, what with—"

"No. Not cut down. Stop. And effective now, not soon, not tomorrow, not anytime other than now. Do you understand me, son?"

"I understand you, Mrs. Lipton."

"And do you agree?"

"Yes. I agree... Okay, well..."

I motion like I'm going to ease past her, but she stands her ground, and cages me in.

"I had no *idea* you drank so much. I mean I knew it was bad, but not... I mean, really, Huckleberry, it's a problem. Red is beside himself. The poor man is terrified. I've just come from visiting with him now and, well, you should see him, see what it's doing to him: he can't eat, can't sleep, he looks terrible, like *he's* got the problem... anyway, he said he'd stay until you were under control, that it was the righteous thing to do." She kisses the rosary again. "He's an old man though, Huckleberry, it's not fair of you to carry on like this, drinking and acting the fool: it's incredibly selfish."

With me sufficiently told, she moves back, and allows me to enter the elevator. I take it up to six, I open my door, and walk inside, and see him.

"Hello, Red."

"Hello, Huck."

"I just saw Lipton—"

"Right, that's what I was going to talk to you about."

"Red."

"Yeah?"

"What happened?"

"So she's up here, right, Lipton, and we get to talking, and one thing leads to another and, before you know it, she's telling me about your drinking—*which* she knows about anyway. She starts saying about how you're always stumbling down the hall, with bottles and cans, making a racket. And anyway, she says you drink a lot, so I just make one of those—what do you call it?—off-handed remarks, like: yeah, I suppose he does... Suddenly she's asking *me* to look after you, says she's tried already, but no luck, and that maybe you'll listen to me... So what am I going say? I say:

sure thing Mrs. Lipton... I say: no problem, count on me... I mean, what was I *supposed* to say?"

"Red."

"Yeah?"

"What happened?"

"So I'm watching porn, right? And there's knocking. So I stay real quiet, but the knocking keeps on, so eventually I stop what I'm doing and answer... And it's her, and I'm thinking fuck me, right? And I'm worrying about: did she hear the porn? I mean, my ears, Huck, they're not too good, so I need the noise up, otherwise I can't make out what they're saying... 'Can I come in?' she says. And now I'm *really* fucked. Because now we're in here"—he sweeps his hands across the living room, the kitchen, at all the bottles, cans—"I didn't want her to think this was all mine, so I say, I say to her that I'm not really a drinker, but that you're an alcoholic, no question, and that it's tragic, and I'll do what I can, but in the end it's your choice, and... Oh hell, Huck, I'm sorry."

"That's okay, Red, I would have done the same thing."

"Still, I'm sorry."

"That's okay."

"Where've you been?"

So I tell him about Milly. Although I don't mention prostitution, nail polish, or that I met her the day after my father died. I still don't feel comfortable telling him about the suicide. Saying it out loud makes it more real, so for now I'm keeping that to myself... In fact, all I tell him is that I was with Milly, and that she is my friend, and that she is killing herself.

"She's a junkie."
"Sorry, kid..." He sighs. "What?"
"Heroin."
He sighs again. "Shit... Sorry, kid."
"Yeah."

We sit on the balcony and stare at the wall. We count the bricks. We disagree on the number. We keep recounting, getting high, never agreeing on the number of bricks. Eventually we give up, concentrate on getting high.

We talk.

And Red asks me if I've ever been in love.

# Chapter 7

### The Diner (take one)

Red is fidgeting. Adjusting, scratching, playing with his tie. What we're doing has got him ruffled. Pissed off, off-color, and itching.

"This is bullshit," he growls, "I mean *really* bullshit." He sighs. "Look, it's not like I'm not here for you. You need something, kid... If I can, I'll do it. But this idea is stupid... I mean really fucking dumb."

"If that's how you feel then back out.'

"You son of a bitch!" he screams. "Don't go accusing me of backing out."

"I'm not, I'm just saying—"

"No one said anything about backing out. No one's backing out of nothing. All I'm saying is this is a dumb fucking idea. That's all I'm saying... I mean, shit, Huck, you've got to admit it's pretty fucking dumb."

He points to his tie, to his jacket. To his slick-back hair. He throws on a plastic smile. He looks ridiculous. *Fuck*.

"So why'd you agree to do it?"

"Two reasons. First, I figured I owed you for Lipton."

"And...?"

"Well, the other thing was I was high."

That gets us laughing, eases the tension. Unties my stomach...

We tip the driver ten and he lets us smoke our cigars. Windows down. I like cigars. Smoking them, but more the way they smell. My shrink said, because my father smoked them. If there was a way to pay cigar prices for cigar smells, I'd do it in a heartbeat. If I were economical, I'd become friends with cigar smokers. And just follow them around...

"Stop," I say to the driver.

"But it's another four blocks," says Red.

"I know," I say, "but I want to get out here... I need a minute to collect myself."

...There is a heavy rain, and the streets are empty. I stand on the corner, Red stands on the corner. As I ready myself a homeless man walks past. Red nods at him. The homeless man does not nod back. He shows no signs of recognizing Red. Red is quiet for a minute. Then he asks me for a hundred dollars. He never asks me for money, so I give it him, and he catches up to the homeless man. He stops him and they exchange words, then Red hands him the money and the man hugs him before shuffling across the street and into a liquor store. Red comes back. We don't talk about what happened. That was Red. Before I fell over him in the alleyway. That was his life.

We walk toward the diner...

Heart racing, everything in slow motion. The door swings open and I step inside. My legs are rubber, I almost fall, Red holds my arm, and steadies me.

*I see her.* I try not to get too excited, and give the game away. But my insides are jumping. And it takes the banking of a million mirror promises not to pull out my flask. Still, I put my hand in my pocket, and massage the pewter. Feel it as it feels me. As it measures me. Tries to call me out. For drunks—pewter is the cunning metal. I pull my hand away.

She looks good. I watch as she brings table four his pie and coffee. Laughing, playing with her hair, batting lashes. A lean over the table. *Is she considering him?* That and a million other jealousies shudder me. Almost make me fold. Almost make me drop to my knees, and beg for another chance. But I don't. Instead, I observe the prospect. *He doesn't look artistic*, I tell myself. *He's not her type.* I relax. *She's just doing it for the tips.*

We get a table. A waitress comes over. She is new, and frayed, and shitting a trail of awkward. I can smell it. She asks us what we want. We order a couple of pieces of pie and some coffee.

She takes forever to scrawl it down, before shifting off, head shaking, flustered. The place isn't nearly as full as it gets, and she's struggling... I know waitresses, really well as it happens. Most of my exes are waitresses. So me saying she won't make it another week is a qualified assessment, not me being a prick... (The turnover is sky-high, a thankless job, for the thick-skinned: shitty pay, tip-reliant.) I decide to leave her a boost, something like double the bill, whatever that comes to. Maybe that'll keep her at it long enough to figure things out. The truth is, I don't do enough things like that—enough good deeds—and I want to make sure this sticks, so maybe I'll triple the tip... or fuck it, maybe I'll leave her a hundred dollars, give her a *real* boost... She comes back with the coffee and pie. The pies are wrong. Instead of apple, twice, we have peach cobblers. I thank her, and throw her a dirty wink. She smiles... And off she goes, thinking she can do this, and that I would *if* she wanted... Of course, I wouldn't. She's not my type. But white lies are essential, they are the hope bricks of the downtrodden. And they must be handed out...

Our table is in the corner. I watch as Rumi scurries around for a couple of minutes—clearing, smiling, serving, eating shit. Then she disappears... And she doesn't come back. I keep my eyes on the prowl, scanning, but nothing. *Cigarette-break, must be. I bet if I went outside for a smoke... But that's not part of the plan*, I tell myself, *stick to the script.*

Ten more minutes drag themselves out... and I am convinced she is being raped in the alleyway. It has been twenty minutes since she disappeared. It takes six minutes for a normal smoker to have a cigarette and she is a fast smoker and I know that right now she's being raped.

I stand up and head out the front. Then round the side. She is there. She is not being raped. She's talking to... I can't believe it. The trucker is right up on her—the one who called her a vagina—and he's whispering in her ear, like he never did what he did... And I get *the fury...* I should have fought him back then, after he said what he said, should have pocketed my cowardice and been a man about things. I've had my ass kicked a lot since then, and I can't help thinking it's karma fucking me over, telling me I should've been a hero. Taken some hero licks...

*The fury. The fury.* My heart is pumping—flooding me with an energy—as I run over, grab his shoulder, twist him round. The alleyway is dark, and I am quick, and I catch him by surprise. I spin him, then connect a perfect shot, right on the nose. I hear it break, and watch the blood spurt. I've landed the big one. I feel joy. I am a shitty fighter. I punch but I never connect right. And I've landed the big one. And I feel joy... I forget about the man with the bloody nose, and just assume it's like the movies: one good lick, and the bad guy exits, and you get the girl...

But then reality—that cruel dream—comes crashing down, burying me in it's vulgarity—all hands and fists, bones and sharp edges—bursting my bubble-gum world, splitting my head wide open, feeling those rivers run. Skin breaking its silence... The long red pour... I watch it, watch it all, from the overhead. Witness from up high—the slaughter, the misery of that poor soul... it's not happening to me, not really. Not after I'm down, and kicked, and beaten hard. Not after my eyes close. They shut and I hardly feel the kicks, the punches, metal. They become only shadows of the actual. I am pain-free...

There is only the faintness of her screaming...

... Now it has stopped... And now I can hear her—my ears, before scurried to safety, return. She is hysterical.

"Oh my God, oh Christ," she is screaming. "Are you okay?"

I sit up, bolt up mechanically, and smile. "I'm fine." I hear my voice. I am casual. "And how are *you*?" I say it cool, like I'm looking to get laid. Like I'm looking to get laid *now* in the alleyway. The inflection, its delivery, startles her, lights her eyes up, and makes them shine. *Fuck*. She has prettier eyes than I remember: gold flecks that I swear are new.

"*I'm* fine," she says. "What are you doing here?"

Before I can answer, she's tugging at my sleeve. "We should call the police. People can't go around doing stuff like that and expect to get away with it. And where did his knuckleduster come from?..."

I tune out, run my eyes over her stockings, imagine myself grabbing her, putting her up against the wall, going hard, going slow, hard, slow, hard, hard... A pull on my arm, and I tune back in.

"... Christ, I didn't think those things *actually* existed, not really. And he was just *wailing* on you like a fucking animal! Jesus..."

She goes on like this for a while (I take out my flask): about society and anarchy, and order, and other stuff, probably; I tune out again, taking comfort in her concern, but not its particulars. When she stops talking, I touch her thigh.

"It's the system."

She nods. "I know people, you know." She says she's going to make some calls, that she knows serious people who'll sort this out. But I convince her to leave it alone... She helps me to my feet. I check that everything works. I'm okay. No breaks. Just swells, and bruises.

We go back into the diner. She tells me I need to go to hospital. I say I will. She offers to go with me, but I tell her no. She kisses me on the cheek, and I kiss her on the cheek, and we look at each other. I don't make the move. I want to. And that's why I don't. Because my instincts are always getting in the way of my progress. Instead I do the right thing. I grab Red, and leave. On the way back home he wants to know what happened to my face... I tell him I took some hero licks. And I laugh. And it hurts. And it feels good...

Back at the apartment, and I search all my clothes, every pocket. I can't find the oxy. I need something. I'm starting to hurt real bad. So I pour whiskey and drain. Pour and drain. Until I get a numbness. Then I sit down with Red, and fill him in.

I tell him a story, an elaborate one, about her in the alleyway and this guy harassing. Invading her space. Maybe trying to rape her. No. Definitely, he was definitely trying to rape her, and I stopped it. I waded in. "He could have had a gun, Red, but I had to do it. I mean what else was I going to do?" It's a good story. The story I tell. And after it Red looks at me different. Like I'm not just a kid with too much therapy, and too small balls. Like I'm an army buddy or something.

"I swear, Red, I was giving as good as I got, maybe I was even a little ahead... but then he started fighting dirty, picked up some broken brick and did this to my face... You know, no one plays by the rules anymore... It's the system."

"Goddamn right, kid. The way the world is—everyone's looking for an advantage."

We drain the drinks. I get up and take the glasses to the counter. I feel good and drunk and happy. I think I have another shot with Rumi. Plus me and Red are doing good. I feel like a kid and I can't stop smiling.

Anyway, I want to stay up and talk to Red. But I can't. I get excited and drink too fast. And I start to slur, and my head hurts, and I'm dizzy. And I tell Red I'm going to lie down, just for a minute. But when I lie down, I know I'm not getting up and I shout to Red that I'm taking a nap. And I pass out...


The Diner (take two)

*The next day. Another cab ride.* My head is shook. I'm not good like this, under pressure. It's the adrenaline: it freezes me up and stops me thinking. I take out my flask and drain it in two long pulls. I need more. But I've had enough. I can't be slurring.

I stare out the window. We hustle down Addison Avenue, toward Wrigley Field. And I can feel the testosterone jamming itself against me. Trying to seep its way in...

I see shouting, swearing, laughing. I see a lot of drinkers and drunks hugging. The Cubs game is on so there's a lot of *that* going on—strictly male love, strictly about the game. Heaven forbid two men just get together over a drink, and get vulnerable. No—it has to be done under a curtain of beer. Under cover of a stadium or sports bar. After a home run. We can't just be honest with ourselves. Can't say: *I love you, man. Thank you for the friendship.* It's a fucked-up world...

We drive past Cubby Bear. And I get a memory jerk. There was a shot girl there two summers ago, and she liked my eyes. "You have the clearest blue, I could dream in them, take me home." And I did. I took her home. Anyway, my eyes were enough to get me a couple of good-time months. My friend—I had friends back then—he liked her too, but his eyes were hazel. "Sorry, I have a thing for blue," she said, when he tried it on. But he wasn't too bitter. She had a friend who wasn't bothered about eyes... How did that end? I don't remember. But it *did* end, and that makes me sad. Often when things end I don't feel a thing—maybe relief, but nothing bad, and then BOOM it hits me over the head when I'm least expecting it: like right now, in this cab. A wave of emotion hits. And I feel like crying. But I don't. Red would go nuts if I did, so I keep it in... That was a good summer, two summers ago. I was one of the guys back then. Before my dad died, and I got serious about being alone... We'd have a good time, me and the guys. We'd play poker, grill out on a porch, a lot of laughs, girls, music, strip clubs. There was always music and girls and a lot of laughs... I think about the shot girl. Christ, what was her name? I rack my brain, and pick out Jen from the possibles. That was it. Jen. She had these emerald eyes, long wavy hair, blonde, big breasts, and a great smile, perfect teeth. She had a little pixie nose that drove me wild. God, she was something... I remember the first date we went on. The only date, actually. Because after that she just ended up coming over after work. And she'd get drunk, and me drunker, and we'd fuck. Unless I got too drunker, in which case, we wouldn't... No wait... her name was Carolyn. Or was Carolyn the Greek girl? Either way—it ended and shouldn't have *because* it was good...

When something gets good it gets taken away, yet the bad always sticks. Why is that? Take California... The number of times I've tried to break it off... But she won't let go. No matter what I do, she clings to me, sticks to me like a stench, like bad fucking luck. No matter where she is, she hovers: texts, phone messages, missed calls—I am constantly bombarded. Electronic shoulder-taps suck out my marrow. Push me further along the ledge... I should never have done what I did. Invited in that trouble... There's a way to deal with the California problem. I know it. I just haven't figured it out. Or maybe I have but I can't remember. For all I know, it's sitting on top of my bedroom cupboard gathering dust. Fading, along with all my best insights... That's where the good stuff goes. All my best lists—I'm a list maker, my best notes are stored up there. Kept safe for later. For when I need them... It's good to know they're up there. Good to know I'm not losing my best ideas. That they're stored and safe and somewhere... When I die, someone will get to the top of my cupboard. Probably some cleaning lady. And she'll have all this knowledge. All my sweat and tears, right there in her dirty black hands. I wonder whether she'll read them, or whether she'll just throw them away... I hope she takes the time to read them. See, I'd like to be remembered, even if it's only by her. I think being remembered is critical...

"Huckleberry...?"

I hear Red's voice.

"Yeah?"

"You okay?"

*No, Red. I'm nervous.*

"I'm fine."

"You were mumbling..."

"I'm fine."

"We're here."

We stand outside the diner...

"Follow the queen, follow the queen, follow the queen, come on people, follow the queen, the queen, the queen, the queen..."

A shell game's being run. Outside the doors an excited crowd gathers. They are witnessing a throwback. I, and probably they, haven't seen a shell game in forever. The government is cleaning things up, policing the fun out of the streets. Everything is permits, licenses. Nowadays, you need permission to beg a living. You need the right forms to run your hustle... "Follow the queen..." The little man—brown, battered hat, loose jeans, bomber jacket—is moving the cards. Across and under. He shifts them, but not too quick. He doesn't want the patsy to think the fix isn't in. There's always one sucker who thinks he can follow the hands, who assumes that's the game... Little man stops, the cards lie still.

"Twenty'll get you forty. Put your money down. Where's the queen? Where's the queen?"

I watch, amused, eyeing up the crowd, predicting the suckers. One of them, banker, lawyer probably—he has that swagger in his shoulders—muscles forward, a twenty in his hand. He puts it down on the cardboard makeshift table. "Middle one," he says, loud, like "fuck you—pay me." Little man asks him if he's sure. Swagger says he is. Middle is turned over. Nine of diamonds. Little man picks up the left, eight of hearts, then the right—and there's the queen. All except one, the crowd laugh. No one likes a lawyer. No one likes a banker. Everyone cheers for the underdog. Little man goes again.

"Follow the queen, follow the queen..."

... I'm better now, the shell game's got me evened out. I turn to Red, "Come on, let's get inside before the police come." He nods. The police will come. They always do. Unless you're being robbed, of course...

This time we sit in Rumi's section. Last time's waitress, the nervy one, sees me come in. I smile, she smiles, I wink. She tries to wink back, seduce me, but it doesn't come off right. More like she's got dirt in her eye. Embarrassed, she looks away, blushed. Still, I watch her, observe as she takes orders, brings coffee, talks to the punters. She's getting a handle on it. The nervy girl, she's becoming a waitress...

"What you smiling at?" asks Red.

"Nothing," I say. "Just that waitress looks more like a waitress than she did last time."

"You're a strange kid."

"Okay."

"You know I don't want to be here, right?"

"Yes, Red. I know." And I don't blame him. He's tired of getting dressed up. Would rather be sitting at home, naked, with a handle, a bag of chips, reading Keats... Did I mention that I caught him reading Keats? Snuck up on him when he figured I was asleep. And I thought real men didn't read. I guess I was wrong... Lipton likes Keats too. And I said that to him. Said that they had that in common. Then I made the wedding bells sound. And he didn't appreciate that. So, I think that means he likes her. Not that he'd ever admit it...

"So explain this again. One more time. So, you told the girl, Rooo...?"

"Rumi."

"Right, Rumi—you told Rumi that you're a writer?"

"Right."

"But you're not a writer?"

"No."

"But you want to be?"

"Yes."

"And you've told her about all these books you've read, these *clever* books?"

I nod.

"But you haven't actually read them?"

"Mostly not, no."

"... even though you *own* the books... *and* you like to read. Am I getting it right?"

"So far, yes."

Red takes a sip of his coffee, plays with his beard.

"Huh," he says. "And you and her were together, so to speak?"

"So to speak."

"And she dumped you because you're a fraud?"

"It wasn't like that. *I* walked out on *her*—emotionally—*way* before the letter."

"What letter?"

"That's not important. And you're missing the point. It didn't work out *because* she called me a fraud. That's what it boils down to, Red. She had the nerve to say I'd never read Kafka. Said I just knew some quotes, to make me look good. Called me a quote-memorizing whore... Look, Red, you shouldn't go around accusing people. Saying hurtful things without proper proof. It's vulgar, and quite frankly dishonest..."

"... *Have* you read Kafka?"

"I have not."

We laugh. Roll around in our seats like children. Unable to breathe, a deep thunderous belly laugh. And patrons stare. That's fine with me. We're having a good old time. Huck's having a good old time for once. So let them stare.

# Chapter 8

Front line reporter

The plan was simple. We go to the diner. Me and my "agent" (Red). Rumi sees us. Comes over. Hears I have a book deal. Feels small. Regrets breaking up with me. And apologizes for saying that I wasn't a writer. Then she begs me to give her another chance. She tells me she loves me too. That was the plan. And it was beautiful. But nothing ever works out for old Huck. Everything's always spiraling and down...

Instead of sticking to script—drowning in self-loathing, feeling worthless—she becomes some kind of a frontline reporter; firing questions, pushing me around, cornering me—showing me she's got the clevers: the ones I knew she didn't have, back when I had her... Green grass, man, fucking karma...

First come questions about the book. Firing thick and fast—*What characteristics does the protagonist possess? How many drafts were there?*

*How do the drafts differ? Do you think the final draft is better than the first? With each new draft does the polish destroy the original edginess? When do you know you're doing more harm that good in the rewriting process?*

Then, when I'm beaten down, she picks me up, pushes me against the ropes, wades in from a different angle—*What kind of deal have you been offered? What is the agent's cut? How did you end up with this particular agent?* She turns to Red. *How long have you been around? Who have you represented? What's your cut?* Red cowers. These are not the questions we'd prepared for. Indeed, we'd not prepared for any questions... And on and on it goes until I'm bright faced, and stuttering, and feeling like I'd wanted her to feel—small and stupid and insignificant... Fucking karma...

"So," she says, "I think we can all agree that you're lying." She eyeballs us both. I look at Red, Red looks away. The game is up, I look down. She turns to Red. "How do you know writer-boy?"

Red sighs. "Met him in an alleyway. We were drunk and got to talking—and he offered me a place to stay." He puts his hand out and touches her arm. "Hey, listen, outside of all this foolishness"—he points to his jacket—"he's a decent guy... Give him a break."

But she doesn't seem swayed. Not thawed by the details of my Samaritan side... No, she seems angry. This wasn't supposed to go like this. This isn't how you win the girl back.

... I want to stick around, make up some other lies, plead my case. But I can't. My bladder's seventy, and I'm feeling the coffee... Lately I've noticed I can't hold it in for more that a few minutes. If I try, I trickle. I am a trickler now, a poster-child for the diaper trade. Today I am wearing light-colored pants, so no wiggle room, a small leak and I'm red flagged, a laughing stock... I get up and excuse myself and head off to the restroom...

Two men in a cubicle: eyes hungry, animal-like. They have yet to close the door. I've caught them in the just before, in the undeniable obviousness. One is small, and my entrance—swearing, crashing doors, loud—startles him, almost tipping him into the toilet bowl. The other is large and angry and has frustrated eyes, glaring coals. I look away, intimidated... Nervous, I forget myself, and, I'm ashamed to say, start to leak. He looks down at the patch, I look down at the patch. We watch it form. It is not my patch, it belongs to someone else, and then the warmth... and then it belongs to me.... I start swearing, tightening up, pinching back my flow. It's hard midstream and I fail and my pants are wet and messy and embarrassing and mine. I hustle over to the sink, cursing my aging; I hear a door close. And then they, who came to do, start the doing... I take off my pants and examine the damage. It is brutal. I grab a handful of paper towels.

Groaning starts and gets louder. I fold the towels and dab. I stick the pants under the hand dryer. It does not work. Groaning gets louder. I pull on my pants. Someone—the big guy, probably—reaches the finish line. I head out the door and back to my table... To more eyes.

One set. She is not there. Only Red sits, tired and drawn and beaten up bad.

"Sorry, kid," he says. "She said she didn't want to know. I tried to tell her how you've looked after me but it didn't seem to take."

"That's okay," I tell him. "Let's go home. I need a drink."

*... A night of oblivion.* Of hurrying to the bottom of one bottle, to the top of the next, to the bottom of that, and on... I am so sad about Rumi, so angry at my mother, so sad about and angry at my father, that I cannot describe it, cannot talk about it. There are too many emotions swirling around, squeezing me... and I cannot drink enough... Red is down too. But I don't know why. He doesn't want to talk. Neither of us does. So we sit in silence. And drink and drink and drink and drink. And no one says anything. And it's like being alone all over again. Like losing everyone all over again.

*Morning.* Red shakes me, gets me up. I am groggy, like always, and sick. I lean over the side of the bed and vomit. A nasty blackness gets into my mouth, bites the back of my throat. Then come the dry heaves. I am not a well man. My body is shutting down. Red asks me if I'm okay. I tell him I'm good. He doesn't say anything. He throws up a lot too...

"You were talking in your sleep."

"Okay."

"About Rumi."

I don't say anything.

"You've got to let that go, kid."

I nod.

"Your phone's been going off. It's been driving me nuts."

"Sorry, Red."

"I'm going into the kitchen..."

"Yes, please."

Red slinks off to get us our drinks.

I check my phone. I have ten missed calls. All from California. I wonder if I answered. And if did, what did I say? Christ, the shit I get myself into. In blackouts, out of blackouts...

Red comes back. I take my glass, a tall glass full of whiskey, put it to my lips, and swallow as much as I can before the convulsions.

Red puts his hand on my shoulder and speaks.

"I'm going away for a little bit."

"Where?'

"I don't want to say."

"Okay."

"I might look for my son."

"Okay."
"Or I might not.
"Okay."
"I might go and see Ed."
"Okay."
"Or I might not."
"Okay."


## Alone with Dylan

This news doesn't upset me. It would if it were true but it's not. Red's said that before. Said he'd go. Normally late at night when we're three sheets. But in the morning he's always there. Snoring, stinking up the place, drinking my whiskey. Being my friend... I finish the glass, convulse some more, and go back to sleep...

And when I wake up Red has gone. *Red is gone. Red is gone. Red is not here. And I feel lost. And I am not prepared. And I feel lost. And Red has gone. And I am sad. I cannot cope, cannot handle... And I need oblivion. Give me oblivion.*

I search every piece of clothing, every hiding space, every corner of my apartment. Until I find the oxy. It is in one of my old hiding places, one I never use, because I could never remember it. In it I find four hundred dollars and oxy. I spend the next week in a bubble...

I listen to Bob Dylan, for seven days straight. I sit in my room and take the pills, the oxy, chop it up, snort it, fold myself into its layers, and fade off. It is something close to God. At least, that is what I imagine; I've never been a Godly man, but I've seen them on TV collecting money—and they seem happy. I drink a little beer, here and there, but not much, and only to keep me hydrated. I smoke cigarettes. Other than the pills, I'm pretty much clean, and quiet, and sober. The oxy leaves me breathless, tongue dripping, and sprawled across my mattress. This is better than booze, better than sex, people, connecting, laughing, feeling, living. This is what it's all about... I do not think about Rumi, Red, mother, father, pain. I do not think about any of that. I only think about Bob Dylan...

"Last Thoughts On Woody Guthrie"—Have you ever *listened* to the words? I mean really *listened* to them. They're the answer, you know—the fucking truth. He's figured it out, put it down in five pages of scribble—read out in his gravely tones, his tired hoarseness; he's been around. You can hear the coffee stains, cigarette stains, life stains. You can hear realness, no angles—*look at my skin, look at my skin crawl*— I've met before, you know, Dylan: loads of times. You ever have that dream where you're with your heroes? He's at my table, sat next to me, not eating, smoking, drinking red wine, writing things on napkins—open-eye words—pocketing them for later... Imagine if you really *did* know him. Wouldn't that be something! I heard he listens to his own records. But so what, right? He's Bob fucking Dylan. I can't remember who told me that—in that nasty way people talk when they're intentions are crooked—but whoever it was can go fuck themselves. It takes real talent to be a critic, real balls.

By the start of the eighth day, I am, I don't know what I am, except wiped out, drained, and out of oxy. I want more, but I don't have the drive to doctor-shop—you know, go around complaining of the right things, hoping to get a bendable ear, a kind scribble... I make a mental note to ask Jimmy if he can score for me. He'll say no, because he always says no, because that's Jimmy, but I'll make it about the math, dollars and cents, and he'll come through. Because he's a businessman.

I go to the kitchen and look for my keys. I don't need them, but I need to find them, need to know where they are. It's my OCD... And I can't find them, can't find my keys, and I am trapped. And I start to cry. But I don't know why. It can't be about the keys. I don't even need them. I have drink and weed and food, and apart from the oxy, I'm fully stocked up. I think it's the pain that makes me cry. Rumi, Red, mother, father. Loneliness. All of it makes me cry. And I remember it all together. I feel all the pain together. And it is too much. And I sit on the floor in front of my couch and wail and wail and wail and wail... and I don't know for how long.

I cry for so long and so hard that by the time I'm done I'm stone cold sober. For an alcoholic that is a scary place, a dangerous place. And I grab a bottle, and tip and pour and heave and pour and pour and pour.... And I don't know why but the drinking that hasn't felt good lately, feels good now... I put on some records, old ones, and sit back, pretend like I'm in a smoky backroom, listening to history *before* they were famous...

The music owns me, and I'm transported to a front table: Ella, Nina, Billie, Joni, Dinah. They don't make them like that, not anymore they don't. That I know their music makes me feel good, because I shouldn't know, because I'm so young. Most music nowadays is dead. Plastic suicide. Suffocating. Airless. Most music today isn't music. I turn up Joni—"A Case Of You"—I feel her pain, her truth... I bet she knew Dylan, *knows* Dylan. I bet he knows her, in the biblical sense. I bet genius is incestuous.

There is a phone call. A call that comes in, vibrates in my pocket, and shocks me. It's a number I don't recognize. But I'm so lonely, I answer it. I have a conversation, I think with California... I think she screamed. I think I cried... I'm listening to Joni, to "Clouds" now.

And I drink too fast. To hide from the pain. And shield myself in the sledgehammer blackness...

And I keep drinking...

Everyday I go to the store. I take the alleyway hoping to see Red. But he is not there. I have only myself. Alone, lonely, hurting, drowning in bottles, I swim deeper into oblivion...

# Chapter 9

Dry

I'm officially done with the booze. It was listening to Joni Mitchell's "A Case Of You" that did it... Songs are powerful. They shake you up. They're motivational building blocks for people like me. For people that size you up wondering *what's your angle?*... See, we, us, the disenchanted—we don't believe you, don't believe your words, your promises, your self-promoting infomercials. *Buy this and you'll look like that. Buy that and you'll be skinny, have white teeth, that smile, these friends...* No, words don't mean shit to people like me. But a song, a real song, an old song, doesn't have an angle, isn't a plug for special interest groups. It's just an emotion. And I can get behind that. I can get behind that big time...

I pour out all my wine, my liquor, my beer. I roll a joint. I sit on the balcony. I get high. I pick up *Factotum* from the shelf. The weight of it in my hand, the texture, the smell, comforts me... At first it is a strange sensation, reading—it's been a while—but soon I've got the cinema screen up in my head, matching images to the words...

The next couple of weeks I am less alone. I have my books... The phone rings. California. It keeps ringing. California. I switch it off and bury myself into the pages. I read Bukowski: *Factotum*, *Post Office*, *Women*, *Ham on Rye*, *Pulp*, *Hollywood*. I read it all... I like his voice, how he writes, his alcoholic hero; I like that he does that—gives a drunk center stage. He says, it's okay to be flawed. He says *it's okay*. It's going to be *okay*... And I read...

And I need to read. Need the words to paint the images to distract me from my sickness... My body is bucking, fighting the detox. It's been two years since my last dry spell—that lasted nine days—and my bones are acting up. They itch. I shake, I throw up, I sweat. I have no appetite. I cannot sleep...

I've done this before. And I hold on. It's hard though, holding on, and a couple of times I almost fold, but I don't. I'll read something funny and I'll laugh and I'll get a shot of *okay* and I hold on. And I hold on and hold on, and keep holding, and keep holding on.

... And I think... Not drinking gets my head going, gets it moving at a million miles; it's a terrifying place, my head, a scary space, especially sober, and the thinking almost gets me to drink...

I think about potential, as I'm shaking, shivering, dry-heaving, sweating. And I realize I hate it—and all that become-a-better-you nonsense, that Oprah drip... That sort of crap is for soccer moms, yogis, chai-latte drinkers; people who converse hands-free, who conference call; people who get hard for PowerPoint, have business lunches, power breakfasts, do Pilates, work their core, cross-train, eat protein bars; people who take hunting trips, have summer homes; people who yawn strategically... people who read self-improvement guides. I can't stand those books, those you're-doing-it-wrong manuals. We are who we are. That's the truth, the bottom line...

And I think... about Hollywood... shaking, shivering, I realize that I'd struggle there. That my aversion to the right endings, to cake-cutter storylines, would scare the moneymen away... *You know what,* I tell myself, *fuck Hollywood*. No one writes the right words anyway. Not when there's money on the line. Independent filmmaking, man, that's where it's at... That's what I realize, shaking, sweating, thinking, holding on...

And I think about that other stuff too. That sad stuff. And people I miss. But when the cloud gets deep and heavy, when it starts to swell, I tune out and think about things like skyscrapers and bridges and planes and how they work... I find a lot of things fascinate me when I'm not drunk. The world gets me wide-eyed in wonderment.

... And it gets better... I'm not completely alone. Lipton comes around two, three times a day. Knocking down my door (she has a heavy fist, bony knuckles), checking I'm alright. She saw me in the corridor coming back from the store—with soda water and Tylenol and no booze—on day two of my detox: when I was in terrible shape. She'd asked me if I was detoxing. And I told her yes. And she smiled and told me she was proud of me... That shouldn't have meant anything to me. I know. But it did. And I don't know how I feel about that. About needing Lipton... Lipton asks about Red. And I tell her the truth: that I don't know where he is or what he's doing. *Do you think he's coming back?* I tell her I don't know. When she hears that she gets sad. So I put my arm around her, give her a tight hug. She thanks me, then tells me I need to take a shower, that I need to start looking after myself... She has a good heart. And I tell her okay.

And I think about writing. About being a writer...


The Shawl

Seventeen days after quitting—the shaking, heaving, vomiting, sweating—they have all stopped... And from the outside I look regular again.

*Another cab ride.* A quiet driver, drives me to a place I don't want to go. But that doesn't stop the wheels turning, the meter turning, doesn't stop us arriving... We pull up outside. I don't get out. I know this is a bad idea, so I stall. I want to go back, back to the safety of my smallness—my bed, my couch, my TV screen—but my voice won't work, so I cannot ask for it. I try to kick-start it several times but nerves paralyze my vocal cords, and I stay silent... The driver stares at me, his eyes firing bullets. He starts to breathe heavy. His black coals bury themselves into mine, and work me over... He tells me to get out, I get out.

I enter. It is dark inside. There are stairs going down. I don't touch the railing. (I never touch the railing—the germs, the germs.) And I trip over and fall, tumble down, land on my face. But it's okay. No one sees... I pick myself up, go to the bar, take a stool in the corner, and order a Coke...

I recognize the bar man. He was on TV once, I'm good with faces. A detective in a cop show. But I don't remember which... They're all the same. The bad guys always get got. Always get nailed... in forty-one minutes, plus commercials. Never earlier, never later. Always forty-one minutes plus a word from our sponsors... He was pretty good, too—the bartender—but the writing sucked. It did him in, relegated him to serving drinks to jerks like me instead of playing number two to a Hanks on the big screen... I don't tell him that though. I don't want to be *that* guy, that *you could've been a contender* asshole... So I just order my Coke, and smile, and pretend that I don't know faces.

Waiting for my drink, the room gets weird. My stomach, my head, it all goes sideways. I run to the bathroom, grab porcelain, throw up, keep throwing up, sweating, watching the room spin...

I stay there a while, on the ground a while, clutching the toilet. A line of spit hangs from my mouth, goes down to the floor. Some people walk in, laughing, talking. They spot me and go quiet. I want to tell them that I'm not drunk, or high. That this is just me—my body, my head—shutting down, but they are gone before I get the chance.

When I get back to my seat the bartender is talking to a couple of young girls. They recognize him from that show. I can tell because they're not looking at him like he's a bartender, but like they're nervous, and giddy, and offering sex... When I get his attention I ask for bourbon. I sink it—it feels right—I ask for another, then the bottle. I drink. I haven't drunk for some time so it feels good, really good, so I keep going...

When I'm steady I turn my chair to face the stage. This is *that* type of bar. A bar with a stage. Full of artists drinking wine, talking Che, talking Marx... I've only been here once before. And that time a girl brought me—trust fund girl, lovely figure, young. I remember we had fun until we argued about Lenin, then we stopped having fun, then she left with someone else. I've done that a lot, you know, lost a lot of sex over conversation... The lights are shining on a microphone. It is open mike, poetry night...

In the spotlight stands a wiry man, straight hair, long and ponytailed, trimmed beard, corduroy jacket, skinny jeans; a hipster... His piece, he announces, is called: If I had a dollar. It is about being homeless, he says. I recognize the jacket, the one he is wearing. I have the same one. It costs four hundred dollars. If Red was here he'd jump on stage, and put a hurt on him—for wearing a four-hundred-dollar jacket and talking poverty—but Red's not here—I look around—nor is anyone like him. There are a lot of expensive jackets here. A lot of four-hundred-dollar pieces masquerading as twenty-dollar gear. There is a lot of bullshit in these seats, a lot of Hollywood... Take the hipster. In ten years he will stop experimenting, and take the nepotism train to hedge fund central, where he will start living the better life. Mark my words. He will grow fat, or he will not because he'll have a personal trainer, but he will ride his liver hard (vodka/scotch), and his heart (coke/Viagra), and womanize, cheat on his wife—who was a nine but is now a six (after kids)—with nines and tens. He will die miserable, and alone, and authentically textbook. He will become his father, and his father's father... I feel sorry for him. He is young, early twenties—he has his whole life ahead of him, and it's already over... That he doesn't know it yet is all he has going for him...

Next up is a girl. She wears a shawl. You don't see too much of that. Not around here. Not since New York... Her piece, she says, is on The Towers. The crowd gets quiet, but nervous quiet, like she shouldn't be talking, not about that stuff, not now, not considering...

Her piece: it doesn't rhyme, doesn't try to, unlike the hipster's. Hers is spoken word. Spoken. Word. Not poetry. It is long, over five minutes. She has it memorized. She says it quiet, shadowing her voice into the microphone. The room is dead. Her stillness carries. Chills. Freezes my bones, my marrow, my inner marrow. There are no words, no whispers. There is no movement: glasses lifted, chairs shifting. Everyone is suspended. And listening. To her power... When she is done she walks off stage. There is no clapping. And then... eruption. We have seen something... and we know it. And it wasn't her words, or not only, or even mainly, but her delivery—the courage, her possession of each word, each piece of a word, like she carved them out of herself, owned how they should be taken...

Fuck. Me.

# The Juice

The microphone looks heavy after that. No one wants to go near the steel. The MC comes out, says "anybody in the room?" but no one steps up. So he starts telling jokes... and it makes me boil... The air still drips with the shawl, her words still hang, still perforate my ears, burn into my mind... And his comedy, his infestation, dilutes, insults her pain...

*And the fury comes over me.* I stand up. I see myself move from the bar, weave through the tables. The liquor steadies me, pushes me forward. The MC sees me approaching and asks me my name. "Let's hear it for Huckleberry..." Two limp hands clap two claps. And stop into silence...

*And now I'm in front of the mike.* The lights from the side highlight and target me. The audience gives me quiet. I reach into my pocket. I take out the paper. The piece is called "She Never Would." And is about California. Opening her mouth and fucking me over. Sending me to the infirmary, jail or the morgue... Yesterday I knew it—I didn't need the paper—but I get these memory freezes. So I'll read... *I am nervous*... I had this voice in my head when I wrote it. It wasn't my voice. It was a good voice: Anthony Hopkins. My voice is shit, high-pitched, panicked, not a reader's voice. *I am nervous*. I tell myself to go slow, say all the words: slow and steady and deeper than myself.

I tell myself not to rush... The audience is good, staying quiet as I get my head right... There is no podium so I cannot lean, hide behind, read from. No stool either. There is just me. I hold up my paper, my hand fails me, shaking, shaking hard. So I breathe real deep, close my eyes, and say *fuck you* to the fear; I get angry with my fingers, and that seems to fuel a calm. I open my eyes. But the fear comes back. It comes back for me, and even harder, and my heart sweats, beats in overdrive—I see her—The Shawl. She is sat where I was, at the bar, her eyes staring intently into mine. And I cannot read without her eyes, take mine off hers: cannot use the paper, the paper that I need for the freezes...

And I hear myself. I hear my voice, calmer, deeper, saying the piece that I wrote—that *I* wrote—to an audience coming down from tasting her. It is not me saying it, but my body, my voice, my words, deliver...

My voice stops... so I must be done. The audience is quiet. A few hands clap. But most don't. No boos though. And I did it. I did the thing that I couldn't do... The MC comes back and says some things. But I do not hear him... I head to the bar...

She isn't there. I order a drink, I scan, she isn't there, my heart is racing, I leave...

I want to come back. I want more of this, more juice. This isn't like coke, pussy, booze. This juice is something different, something else, something better... And I need more. More. More... I will go home, write. And keep writing. Become a writer and write *the great book*...

# Chapter 10

Writing

The great book is proving impossible to write. For several weeks now I have sat in my apartment, waiting for the wheels to start their turning. But nothing. Instead I spend my days watching a military procession of ants glide effortlessly in one uninterrupted line of silk across my kitchen wall. They are very impressive, very Chinese. Their lines, their organization, their philosophy show a singleness of purpose, a collective tunnel vision, and I envy them... At times I consider a boiling water cleansing, but clued up on karma, I restrain myself.

Instead I decide to relocate, certain that the trick to unlocking my creative door is to find the key location, the right spot...

I try a coffee shop. Because they're overly cliché, ironically cool. It takes a while to find one that's not part of a chain, but when I do, I walk in, order an espresso, take a seat in the back, where it's quiet, take out my tools—pen, paper, pencil, marker, ruler, staple gun, paper clips, clipboard, file folders—and wait for inspiration...

I tune in to the conversations around me.

... To my left I have a couple, boy and girl, about eighteen. He's going for a look—dreadlocks, black nails, eye shadow, facial piercings, Smiths fucking T-shirt—trying to sell how cool he is, how lucky you'd be if he fucked you, if he let you suck his tongue. *And I get a jolt of the fury.* Not for him, not really, but for the way that works on girls, they always seem to lap that up... Like this girl: she's falling all over herself, begging to drop her panties. It makes me sick. I watch his mouth move, spouting the bullshit that gets you there. "I mean, my dad used to run with The Stones, not that that means anything, of course, but it kind of does if you sit down and think about it, but like whatever." Christ. I hate The Stones. They're just a poor man's Doors. But women, man... women cream themselves for Jagger... Like this girl now: I can feel her heat. The boy does too. He stands up, takes her hand, and leads her into the cubicle marked disabled... I hear giggling, then moaning, then finally groaning. He comes out first. She tidies herself up, texts her friends, or whatever it is that girls do after... He looks over at me, sees me looking back, and nods the tight nod. I nod it back. He's no patsy. When he's done with the makeup, eyeliner, dreads, he'll do well for himself, make the good money, maybe even run things.

... I tune in to a different table, the one to my right. The guy—average build, height, looks—is sat there and having a tough old time. He's meeting his girlfriend to "talk." Right now he's on his own, practicing lines, nervous to go live. He's breathing deep, *real* deep. That's a conscience right there. That's what's fucking him up, causing him to hyperventilate... I feel sorry for him. Me, I've never had a problem telling a girl goodbye. If I'm being honest, and I am, I get high on the relief. I'm telling you, man, a decent break-up, on your own terms, and you're as good as new, and ready to go again... She walks in... She isn't hot. She's a six. He's a five, so for him she's a win, but to me her nose is too big, her eyes too close together, her eyebrows over tweezed. I need a seven, a seven minimum, because I'm an eight, and eights can't go lower than a seven—not if it's going to work they can't, not if it's not about the money or a desperate need to settle... I look at her face: she doesn't know. She smiles, throws her soon-to-be ex doe-eyes, kisses him on the lips, whispers that she loves him. "I love you too," he says, because he has to, because she said it first, because it's what they say now, because they're a couple. Then he excuses himself, turns away, his smile erased; a sheet of dread draining his life force replaces it.

With what little he has left he walks to the counter, orders drinks, comes back, sits next to, not opposite, moves close, puts his arm around her, throws her a nervous smile, a last smile. *And then, deep breath in.*

"Listen, babe, let me start off by saying how wonderful I think you are. Lord knows I've put you through the wringer. You've stuck by me through some stuff, Christ there's no denying that, however there comes a time in any venture when you have to step back, reevaluate your position. And, well, I've been doing a lot of that lately—taking stock, costs and benefits—all standard stuff—and as it goes, and in conclusion: we're over... Wow, that was really difficult, and I wasn't sure I'd have the courage to do it, but I guess you never know how strong you are until—"

He sees it too late. A clean left-hook across his nose, the sound of breaking, blood. She goes in for another, swinging wildly, but he has his arms up now, and protects himself from his... *damn...* from his now ex-fiancée: the sun catches her left fist, lighting up the carats... This, ringside, is too close to the action, too dangerous for me—my heart is racing at a million miles an hour—so I pick up my belongings and move to the front... I take a seat at the window and watch the drama unfold at safe distance. I don't want to get dragged in, catch a stray bullet... I see hugging, crying, consoling, shouting, more crying, and one final punch. And then it's over. She slams the ring on the table, mentions his mother, his broken dick, then leaves... He waits ten minutes, until it's safe, or he thinks it is, then he makes his way to the door... As he walks past, he stops, turns and faces me. "Enjoy the show, dipshit?" he asks. I feel like a coward, pretending not to know that he's talking to me, but I feel extra scared today, more than usual, and I couldn't handle a fight, not even a few punches, so I keep my head down, and pretend to be engrossed in my work. And he lets it go, but only after he calls me a pussy. And the whole place hears, sees me for what I am.

I feel like such a loser, backing down like that. But I do my usual, I block it out. I turn my attention back to my work... I stare at the page. It is blank, still... I wonder, again, how it gets done. I mean, it can't be *that* hard. My head tells me these amazing stories. Surely the rest is secretarial...

I spend the rest of the afternoon uninspired, people-watching, sipping coffee, eating crumb cake. By closing, I have drunk thirty dollars of espresso, and written a dirty limerick... I leave the coffee shop, jittery and with a splitting headache... On my way back home, I stop off and buy ant killer. The good kind, I go for the expensive stuff, the name brand. I go home and apply liberally. I spray the skirting boards, the kitchen floor, the walls... I do not hate the ants, just the ant problem, but I stick around to watch them die, and they do die, and their dying makes me sad... And I bet I could have saved a lot of lives if I had bought the cheaper stuff. And I feel like such a loser, such a genocidal maniac...

Today's efforts have emptied me out. (I don't have many more in me. These kinds of days are coming thick and fast. And they'll get me soon. I'm sure of it.) With all the energy I have left, I plant my feet on the coffee table, switch on the box, flick through the channels... My feet stink, they always do. I can't seem to get the smell out: different soaps, scrubs, nothing works. So I sit here, and smell, and feel sick with it too. In the end I have to put my shoes back on—just so I can sit with myself... I stop when I recognize someone from something old, something good, doing something new, a spin-off maybe. I start watching... It is bad. I can see the jokes coming at me. The writing is sluggish, regurgitated, predictable. But the worst of it is they use these laugh machines. *You should be laughing here, and here, and here, and here... and if you're not, you're just not getting it...* What happened to funny? Did we use it all up? We used to have good TV, when did it end? I hear myself ask these questions out loud, to nobody, to an empty room, reminding me that I'm short on friends, that I'm zeroed out, pathetic... I roll a joint. I'm pretty sure I smoke weed because I'm lonely. If I had friends I wouldn't bother.

Probably I'd be too busy having a good time to notice I wasn't high... I switch off the box, get paper, pen. I am going to write about suicide, a poem. I'll get my words right, go back to the bar, the one with the stage, read again, get appreciated... Then I'll be on my way to a fistful, two fistfuls, fuck it, bundles of high-quality friendships. Then I won't feel bad about missing my old friends. Because I'll have needed to have dumped them anyway to make room for these better ones. Ones I never would have found if: I hadn't gotten rid of my old ones, become suicidally lonely, written about it, and attracted new friends as a consequence... See, that'll be karma working *for* me, for a change. And about goddamn time, too... I sit, pen poised, waiting. *Come on,* I tell myself, *I need my moment*, my "Last Thoughts On Woody Guthrie"... One hour. Nothing. Two hours. Nothing. Three hours. Nothing. No moment. No nothing. I want to punch Bob Dylan, smash him right in the face. I would if he was here. Probably I'd get beat up though. He looks like he can handle himself, Dylan, looks like he can take a punch, throw a punch, fight good, fight better than me, at least... In the end I give up. I switch the box back on. Flick. Flick. Flick. Settle... Two guys and a girl, and one guy is cooler than the other guy, and the less cool guy likes the girl, but the girl likes the cooler guy, but the cooler guy has no idea, and it's all a big clusterfuck. It's not funny. Not that you'd guess, not if you didn't know about the laughter machine, about its propaganda... I reach for my papers, roll another, mute the sound, and subtitle. I read along... and get a bit of hope in me. *If these idiots can make it,* I tell myself, *then I'm on easy street...* I smoke another, the last of it, I get a knot in my stomach. Boy, do I hate seeing Jimmy. But he has the medicine—the stuff I need to write the right writing—so I grab my keys, my wallet, hail a cab, promise the driver an extra ten to fill me in on the world... I never watch the news. I have too much of the cloud to take on extra. Not that it would help them, me knowing. It's just being nosey, if you ask me. Nosey repackaged as informed. Repackaged as concerned... Today though, I feel like a bit of a snoop, so I ask the driver for the ABCs. *Lots going on in India,* he says, *lots going on.* Then he tells me about it...

By the time I get to Jimmy's I feel goddamn depressed. And I wonder if the cloud will ever lose its hard-on for me... I sign in, take the elevator up, walk to his door.

# Chapter 11

Californiə home

Jimmy opens up, naked. His bits, swinging wildly, stare at me, forcing me to stare back. I am uncomfortable... I do not trust the over-sexual. I feel like they're *too* open, as if their vulgarity is a distraction to the monster secret they're trying to hide... The anxiety seeps in. My nervous twitch rears its head. My right eye starts to wink, starts to flap uncontrollably... Jimmy starts to pant. He goes red, clutches his chest. He looks like he's in trouble. *He's having a heart attack*, I tell myself... And I take it personally; I just want to pay and go, avoid anything dark, anything heavy... People are always doing that—doing what Jimmy's doing to me right now: putting you in a tight spot, holding you hostage. They're always putting your feet to the fire, burning your fucking soles... *Stay at home*, I say. *Stay at home and safe and out of the way*... My instincts tell me to bolt—to turn, run, never come back, find a new Jimmy—but I fuck up and freeze... Turns out he's out of breath. And not dying after all... Good news, I suppose.

He scratches his balls and fixes me hard.

"You staring at my work?"

"No."

"Because from here it looked like you were staring at my work."

"I wasn't staring at your work Jimmy."

"I've had my work stared at before... and that's what it looked like."

"Well I wasn't."

"Wasn't what?"

"Wasn't staring."

"At what?"

"At your dick."

"But you had a quick glance though, right? Like when you're taking a leak, and there's a guy next to you going... you telling me you've never had a look across? Is that what you're saying?"

"Jimmy, look..."

"'Jimmy, look' nothing. Don't do that... listen..." He comes closer, to within an inch. I am scared to move my hand. "Just be a man, and admit it: just say, 'Jimmy, it wasn't sexual or anything, but my curiosity got the better of me and I had a quick check just to see what you were carrying.'"

"Jimmy, you're being nuts, now if I can just come—"

"... the words, Huck. The words or you're no longer welcome. And I mean it, I'll revoke your privileges, and this time it'll be for keeps... I'm not fucking about, Huck. Don't force me into a corner. *Don't* you do that..."

He motions with his hands for me to proceed, so I do. I tell him I was checking him out, even though I wasn't... Jimmy may be mentally unbalanced, agoraphobic, paranoid, annoying, but he is also my supplier, which makes him right... And if you're not getting my point, then you're not a fiend... What we—junkies, stoners, addicts, fiends—what we fear more than anything is getting cut off. Meaning the Jimmys of this world can pull their dick hanging in the wind, Joe Pesci bullshit, and we have to sit there. And to take it. We have to smile like *we're* the assholes and take it up the shitter... It's enough to make you murder...

... When he is sufficiently satisfied—when I have debased myself enough for his viewing pleasure, when I have no integrity left to crush—he invites me in. So that he can take my money and my thanks... Dealers have a good gig, man, a good fucking gig...

I enter the living room.

*Fuck.*
Everything stops—my blood, clocks, life, everything. California is here. On the couch, a magazine, smiling.
I cannot breathe, cannot move.

Voice one says *he knows*.
Voice two says *he doesn't know: you'd be dead if he did*.

In the elevator down I feel *the fury*. What happened to *five thousand dollars and you'll never see me again*? People don't keep promises. It's a fucked-up world.

The cab ride back gives me a loud African driver, listening to African radio, talking loud on his African phone. I ask him for quiet, he doesn't understand. But when I tell him to shut up, he understands, starts shouting at me, telling me I should shut the fuck up. I say it back. He stops his car, tells me to get out. I apologize, throw him twenty, he throws it back, and orders me out... So I'm on the street. A pound of stinking weed, nervous, sweating... I can feel the police, feel them coming for me. Somehow I manage to get a cab without losing my shit... The new driver stares at me in his mirror. "You need to get to a hospital, son." He'll take me, he says, no charge. I tell him no... I listen to California's messages, the ones I'd saved and not listened to... *She is: coming back... almost arrived... fully back in town...* No longer numb, I shake with angry, nervous energy. I ask the cab driver to pull over. I open the door, drop to my knees and vomit as an old lady and her dog slide past. The woman looks away in disgust. But not the animal. He tilts his head to the side, curious, and lets out a small sound. *What's the matter, pal? You look like shit.* "Fuck you," I say, loudly. That startles the old lady. And I feel bad about that. But I need to get home. So I close the door and tell the driver to drive on.

## Stella

At home, I decide that I'm too rattled to write. So I make my way to the artsy bar, to look for The Shawl... From that one reading I can tell she has a shine about her. Like she's a good fix. The kind I need. The kind I need *bad*... I want her to know that I'm interested. See if she feels the same... You're probably thinking *that boy's insane—a girl like her would never be seen with a guy like him.* But that's just naive. Except in rare cases, women, even the best of them, just want to be held. And they'll sell themselves short to get at that warmth. Meaning, while it may look to the world like I have no chance of landing her, I'm actually closer to even money... *if* we run into each other again, and if someone, or something else (like religion), hasn't gotten to her first...

Down the dark stairs once again. I put my aversion to germs on hold, grab the railing to prevent another tumble... I don't see her straight off, so

I sit at the bar, at the end, and order a beer... I wait for my eyes to adjust then I survey the room. I cannot see her. And I do a lot of cursing. A lot of swearing into my glass... I need another drink... I signal for the bartender but he doesn't see me. He's busy talking to underdeveloped girls, either underage or bulimic—the look is the same. The girls are smiling. Eager to slide their panties down, their legs open... They're drooling over his Hollywood. Really lapping it up. *A surge of admiration, with undertones of envy.* I bet he gets laid all the time. Probably doesn't even try, just a flash of his smile, a name drop, and he's golden for the lay...

A girl grabs my attention. I see her as she takes to the stage, to a spattering of applause. She is smiling the expectant smile of a somebody expecting applause. Of someone used to the attention. The face is half-familiar. Not quite famous, but almost. I'm guessing TV actor. The world has too many shitty actors. And I am not impressed... The crowd is though. People stop talking, the crowd hushes to silence... (The bartender sees me, I order another beer.) *The piece*, she says, *is called FYI: I CRY I CRY I CRY.* I think that's funny—the title, I mean—so I laugh my loudest laugh. And a bellyful of machine-gun fire sprays the silence, cuts the air, stops her starting... I am the only one. No one else laughs, no one sees the funny...

She reads the piece... It rhymes. And makes no sense. And is very bad... But somehow the crowd doesn't see it. They erupt, a standing ovation...

I sigh... This is the world, right here. We are billions of tasteless drones. Cue the laugh machines. Cue telling me what to like, hate, love, find funny. Cue telling me what to think and why to think it, so I can say so and be right at parties. The right parties though. Cue telling me what parties are the right parties for me... And on it goes... This is a world full of plastic people. And the air is all used up. And there is no more air. No more air...

There is a tapping on my shoulder blade. A woodpecker irritation, gnawing at my bone. I turn around. FYI is standing there. Smiling. She is smiling at me.

"That was you, right?

"Huh?"

"The guy who laughed at the title?"

"Listen, I'm just here for a drink. If I offended you, then..."

"Stop talking."

"Huh?"

"Stop. Talking."

"Okay."

She calls the bartender over. Unlike me she doesn't seem to be outside his peripheral vision.

"Yeah, Stella?"

"Two whiskies."

The glasses come. They get drained. Two more. Two more after that. At some point the bottle gets left. And we pour our own... I wonder if we will sleep together. And I *mean* sleep. I'm very lonely. *Really* lonely.

She gives me her bio as I watch her legs. She has pretty feet. Painted pink toenails. Girl's feet. She is a TV actor like I thought, on a bad and popular television show. I've never watched it. And I say so too. I tell her that I'd heard it was crap though. She laughs at that, calls me refreshing... Her name is Stella, and she likes to tell jokes, and I have a good laugh, and I'm pretty funny when I need to be so I have a good shot of making it to the mattress... At some point she stops laughing and tells me she's an alcoholic. I don't know how to respond to that. So I tell her I think her poem was shit. That makes her laugh...

It gets hazy after that... The next thing I know she's yelling at me, calling me a son of a bitch, saying that I'd said things, bad things. I don't remember saying anything. And I say that too. She says I'm a liar. She slaps my face, she makes a scene. People stare, the bartender sighs, I apologize. She tells me to go fuck myself, she walks away and up the stairs. She is gone. And I do not chase her. I ruin things. That's my M.O. and I do not chase after her.

I pay the tab, I take a cab, I go home.

Eyes three-quarter closed, out of focus, depressed, drunk, I climb across the walls of my corridor. Left and right, I weave. I am unsteady and thirsty and hungry for food. I don't remember the last time I ate. I stop, pause, put my hands under my shirt, feel my ribs, feel their rungs calling out my sickness. The cold air on my torso brings up a coughing spree and I vibrate and fit and wheeze... When my chest eventually settles, I wipe the spittle formed at the sides of my mouth, and across one cheek, and carry on down the corridor, meandering right and left, using both walls to guide me toward 606... Where I will turn my key, enter, and be alone... Fuck, I hate my money. Having it means getting it won't make it any better. And that knowledge, instead of setting me free, digs my depression a deeper trench.

# Chapter 12

The architect

I decide to be a modern writer, maybe the first. This concept of beginning, middle, end, that shit is dated. And people are changing the channel. Nowadays everything is measured in nanosecond sound bites. You have to grab their attention *before* they blink. Or else you've lost. You become white noise. Another failed writer, working in a coffee shop, talking about trying to find an agent that gets him. I want to make it big, I want the car, the driver, the golf club membership, the skiing trips, the hookers, the coke, the fame, the right table. I know I've said I don't care about that shit—or maybe I didn't say it directly, maybe I just hinted at it—but the truth is I *want* to sell out. And I want to do it big. I want everything, all of it. And I'll prostitute my soul to get it.

And I know I can do it too. Back when I was social, my friends would tell me I should write a book. *You've a funny way of spinning things, Huck. You're a funny motherfucker.* I could walk into any

Chicago bar and by closing time I'd have half the place in funny-tears. I'd spin them some stories and they'd forget about their bills, cancers, spouses, jobs. I was magic with an audience. I was God.

For seven days I sit on my couch. I close my eyes and imagine I'm in a bar. I drink and pretend I have an audience; and I push the funny button in my head; and tell myself to make everyone laugh... But it's all bullshit. I don't say anything funny. Most of what I say is angry-drunk rambling. A lot of my sentences don't even make sense... And I worry that I am losing my mind...

The voice in my head calls me a loser... I can feel the depression coming. A tidal wave of sadness heading right for me. By now I can gauge the intensity of these things before they hit and I can tell this one is going to land low and long and hard... I know the booze won't help. I've tried drinking through it before. It doesn't work. Even if I live in blackout, the sickness in my mind stays clear...

*Die, go on, be a man, do it.* I run a bath. I get in with my knife. I sweat. The end, the idea of it, makes me feel relieved, but anxious too. I want to go. And I would. If it wasn't so final. That's the only reason I haven't gone yet. I look at the knife, at the edges. I imagine pushing it into my heart. The battery stopping, pain stopping, one final breath. And maybe regret. It's that fear of regret—of thinking, when it's too late, that I've made the wrong decision—that keeps me from taking off. At least for now...

*A chill burns through me.* But if it's in my genes...? I wonder if I have a choice. If at some point my DNA will take over and I'll have no say in the matter... I have to believe that's what happened to my father. That he wouldn't have left me alone on purpose.

I throw the knife across the bathroom. *Fuck you mom. Not today.* My phone beeps. Text received.

*I don't remember all that much. I laughed. I remember that. I remember it because people aren't funny. So I don't laugh much. But you are funny. Which is cool... I slapped you. I remember. Why. I don't know. I've thought about it. A little bit at least. And I don't remember the details so the way I see it maybe you deserved it or maybe you didn't. Who knows. Either way, I'm not apologizing just in case you did... Anyway, I didn't mean to say any of that but basically if you want to get together and NOT talk about who said what and just get drunk and no fucking just as friends then come down to the bar. Hurry up. I'm already there. My friend stood me up so I'm calling you. Just being honest. THIS IS STELLA BY THE WAY.*

I get dressed. Five minutes ago I was in my bathtub, trying to negotiate my mind around a

sideways slice, now here I am looking forward to a friend-date with a beautiful close-to-famous girl, and all I can think about is her legs, and what jeans to wear. There is something seriously wrong with me. I wash my face, shave, comb my hair, put on jeans and a T-shirt, listen to Nina Simone's "Sinnerman" (or half of it: it's a ten-minute track and I get nervous that she'll get impatient and leave so I turn it off halfway through), grab my keys, text her I'm coming, and head out the door...
I meet two rampant homosexuals in the hallway. T-shirts tied up, bellybuttons exposed: that level of gay. I'm looking good—and I know it—and they want to talk. I tell them I'd love to catch up, just not right now: I'm late for a date. The bigger one, they are both big but the bigger one, blocks my way, and doesn't let me pass.

"Who's the lucky guy?" he says.

"Tobias," I say.

"Serious?" he asks.

"Nah. Just some donkey-dicked sailor I met a couple of weeks ago."

They both smile.

"It's not funny. He needs to get checked out. The condom broke."

"Okay."

"... and I have all sorts."

"Oh."

They stop smiling. I guess that'll put a stop to the eye-raping I get from the building's homosexual element. I don't know why I didn't think of it before. Maybe on some level I liked the validation. Yeah, that's probably it.

I take the elevator to the ground floor, admiring myself in the mirror on the way down. I bump into Mrs. Lipton on the way out. She starts to say something about Red but I'm in too much of a hurry to stop so I brush past her, out the door, and hail a cab.

The cab driver is a happy man. He has a happy wife and three happy children. He was an architect in Pakistan but here he drives a cab. He earns money to send home. He loves America. He is saving to bring his family here. "Sneak them in," he says—his finger over his lips, like: this is our secret. I give him the nod, like: I won't tell anyone... As much as you can know a man without knowing him, I know this man. He is a good man. He is the man I would have been, if I had been a better man... Moved, I tell him to pull over. I go to the cash machine. I withdraw... well, I won't tell you how much—I do not want to dilute my goodwill—but I withdraw a tidy sum. I get back into the cab and drive on to the destination. I do not hear what else he says. I am high on the feeling of what I am about to do... We get to outside the bar and I am shaking with excitement. He tells me the fare and I hand him the fare.

"Nice to meet you," he says.

"Nice to meet you too," I reply. I extend my hand and he goes to shake it and when he does he feels the bundle of notes.

"What is this?"

"It's for your family," I say.

He stares at the money.

"No sir, I couldn't possibly..." he starts. But I hold his shoulder with my hand, to stop him, and he stops.

"Listen, my friend—I am not a good man. There is a sickness inside of me that stops me being good. I do not blame myself. That's just the way I'm made. But I want to do this. Do something that's not for me, perhaps as a first step on the ladder of change; to become someone I want to be, someone I can live with." I hesitate. "Because a lot of the time I do not want to live. Do not take this for yourself. Or even for your family. Take it for me. To help me... Please."

I enter the bar. I feel good. I decide to tell no one what I've done. If I do I know the feeling will leave me... I see Stella in the far corner. A group of men crowd her. She's telling a story and the men are laughing, pretending that they find her interesting. Men are so obvious... I sit out of sight, order a drink and watch. The group is four strong: square jaws, power suits, swept-back hair, bankers probably. They have a self-assured smugness that travels through the air. Their presence, not just here, but on this earth, I take personally. It stings me to know they exist. That they inhale air I do not need, eat food I do not require... I sip my drink and consider my hypocrisy. I chuckle. I think about all the women *I've* smiled at, consoled, befriended, held—all the women I've hustled with my eyes and lies. I am *those men* that I hate so much. We are all the same. All men want—and I mean *all* of us, unless we are defective—is to conquer, to cum. If I were a woman, I'd be a lesbian...

Stella has seen me, and has been trying to beckon me over for a couple of minutes, but I've been enjoying the show so I pretend not to notice until now... I stand up, drain my glass and make my way over to her. When I'm ten feet away, she gets off her stool, walks through the four-pack, and wraps her arms around me. She squeezes me like I'm somebody important. The men, having put in the groundwork, do not like my late arrival.

"Who's your friend?" says the squarest jaw of all, the big alpha.

"This, Charlie Charles, is the love of my life, the man I am going to marry, my fiancé Billy Wilson."

She turns to me. "Bill, these gentleman have been absolutely brilliant, buying me drinks, laughing at my jokes. But really they're just hoping to get into my knickers... The self-assured one, Charlie, thinks he's in with a shot. What do you say, Charlie, am I a liar?"

I smile, but not too loud because there are four of them, and they've been drinking... and I'm a shitty fighter.

My boy Charlie grins. He's schooled enough to know that entering into a conversation with a firecracker like Stella—who has just made it clear she will *not* be banging his brains out tonight—is futile; and like a pro he politely wishes us a pleasant evening, before heading off with the other three mini-alphas in tow. I hear the words "cunt" and "cock-tease" as they fade away.

"Bill Wilson... really?"

"What? Oh... they wouldn't know. Or if they did they wouldn't let on... too proud. Defeat and jawlines do not mix. Take you for instance." She trails her finger across my chin and up the side of my face. "You have great structure so you're totally fucked."

"Fucked?"

"Yeah, fucked: if you ever *wanted* to quit drinking you wouldn't be able to."

She orders a bottle of bourbon, we sit on stools and shoot the shit, two headless chickens grinning it up. Until I'm tired of smiling. I let my face slacken, relax into its natural melancholy.

"What's wrong?"

"Nothing."

"Your face...?"

"I've decided that I'm not going to try and fuck you... I'm not saying I'd be successful—or that you'd want to—only that I'm not going to try... So I don't feel the need to show you that I'm having the time of my life."

"What's the matter? Is it the company?"

"Nope. Your company is good. I'm just generally sad and lonely."

"Even when you're with people?"

"*Especially* when I'm with people."

There is silence for a while. And I'm okay with that.

"Huck?"

"Yeah?"

"You don't like yourself very much, do you?"

"No, Stella. I don't."


## Five never four

I wake up in my bed, alone. I cannot remember last night—nothing after I told her I didn't like... I wince at the memory. I wonder what happened to Stella, with her quick tongue and vulnerable eyes. I hope I didn't do anything stupid. Sometimes the drink brings *the fury*. And I can't control *the fury*. And I hope she's okay.

I roll to the side and put my feet on the floor. My head is a mess. I get naked and stand under water so cold it burns my skin. I try to shake my sickness off. I throw up again and again... something grips onto my stomach, in the worst way. I hold on to the wall, eyes closed, begging for a break in the pain. But none comes. I watch the bile and vomit disappear around my feet, and down the drain, as glimpses of last night flash across my eyes. There was another bar. Then a strip club. And I did cocaine. I can still feel its shake on me. Its dirty jitters scream for a morning drink to wipe it from my body bank.

I walk to the 7-Eleven. I need booze, antacid, full-fat Pepsi. I know I should make a run to the discount store but the coke has me too insecure for cab driver conversation, and the shake of the road will attack my stomach lining and make me throw up.

I put on a fresh shirt, comb my hair, chew chewing gum. I look at myself in the mirror. Apart from the eyes, I pass for together. I put on shades to hide the honesty. I grab my keys and leave my apartment. I hold my breath as the elevator door opens. *Empty.* I ride it down. Again I get lucky. I see no one. I leave the building, breaking right, walk the block to the store, enter, hear that dirty ring, grab water, Pepsi, antacid and head to the counter. Without looking up, I ask for five bottles of Jack. I don't like Jack but they're never out it. Jack is reliable. Jack is loyal. So Jack is what I drink.

"How you doing today, boss?"

It's Tom. Not Asher. Asher is out back, probably looking at child porn, planning an abduction, grooming some nine-year-old on the internet. Sick fuck. I know people. I know he's got a bad tilt. You watch. He'll be on the ten o'clock news one day and everyone else will say: *I didn't know, I had no idea. Seemed like such a nice young man, a quiet boy.* I'll be the only one who knew. That's my skill, you see: I read people.

"Fine," I reply.

One day I'll be in one of my moods and it won't be Tom serving. It'll be him, the kiddy fiddler. And I'll just lose it, become my vigilante other-self. *The fury* will bring the real me out one day, just you wait. And I'll stab him with a pen—again, again, again—until he's dead dead dead. Joe Pesci did that in *Goodfellas*, and people respected him after—despite his height, his comedic face. Violence gets you to the top of the pile. Anger gets you your credit. Mark my words.

I hear "you forgot your change again," but I'm already out the door, trying to balance that fifth bottle and stop it from smashing. I always decline the carrier bag. And almost always lose bottle five on my way back. Then watch as it hits the sidewalk and shatters, the sound of the breaking, the shards looking up at me, calling me a cunt. I don't know why I decline the bag, or why I buy five bottles instead of four. That's just my way, I suppose. Making life difficult, tipping the odds against me. Just to get my juices flowing, convince me I'm not quite dead... yet... Today there were no accidents and I get upstairs with all five intact.

## Woman-fever rollercoaster ride

I get a good half-bottle in me before woman-fever gets its claws in.

Then I can't help but think about Cali. Boy, could she do sex. Brother, was she the best. I think because she has evil in her. She must do. She fucks like she's possessed. There is no *no* with Cali, no *we shouldn't, we couldn't, I can't...*

And I think about Milly too. Fuck, does that make me sad. Seeing how she's got. How's she's sliding down. A quicksand doorway dragging her into hell. Jesus. She'll be gone soon. Which is why I don't want to see her. I want to remember her how she was. Not how she was before. When I first met her. No. But how she must have been—how my head tells me she was—when she was little. Before life and men like me, worse than me, fucked her up, got her on the main line, shooting dope, being a fuck-doll junkie...

And my mom. I think about her. That's where all the fury's from. Why I have so much hate in me. I hate her, wish she was dead, wish I could kill her. Do you know what that's like—walking around with the knowledge that you want your own mother dead, that you want to do the killing? Fuck...

Then there's Rumi. I don't know how I feel about her anymore. I know I had an interest brewing. But I'm hot and cold. Hot and cold. And that might have gone. No, that *has* gone. Probably left when Red left. No, more likely when I met Stella. When she caught my eye, when I started to obsess on her. That's how it normally works: new girl takes away old girl pain.

Stella. My current head-squeeze. I know we said "just friends" but that's only because she said it. Meaning I'm playing the long game, meaning she better watch out... I should text her though. Otherwise she'll forget I'm around. I know girls like her. They're very in the moment. Very hard to pin down. I pick up my phone.

*Text 1—13:04*
*Hey Stella, what a night huh?!! Good times. Terrible head this morning. Needed a cold shower and some whiskey just to wipe it off. Anyway, just wanted to make sure you got home safe. This is Huck by the way.*

I sit staring at the phone, waiting for the beeps, for a message—with hopefully an *x* at the end of it (*x* to signal that maybe I have a shot, and to keep trying). But nothing comes. Not even a *good morning* or a *fuck you, Huck*... The pain is bad. Pretty bad, not unbearable, but almost, as it always is, as it always must be when you put yourself out there to be rejected. See, that's why I don't do *this*. Because of feelings like I'm having now... To take my mind off of my phone I decide to tidy. First, I do a sweep for bottles and cans. I fill up two big black bin liners. And still the place looks like a drug den. Next I do the dishes. I work like a meth head and get everything meticulously clean. I have a dishwasher but no dishwasher soap so I do it all by hand, no gloves. So my hands burn. And it's a good burn, an alive burn, and it feels good. Next I try hoovering. But my hoover is broke. Or the bag is full. Either way, I go over dirt and nothing budges. I put the hoover away and do it all by hand. I get down on my hands and knees and with kitchen towel I wipe the kitchen tile. I use a brush for the carpet and that works pretty good, although it takes a while and cramps my wrist. Next I do the windows. I use regular soap to wash them. Then I do the toilets, the bathtub, change my bed sheets, put all my clothes in black bin liners to take to the laundry... I look around. The place looks okay. Not good but not like before either. I check my phone. 15:58. She hasn't texted back. I figured she would've texted back by now. But then I remember she's one of *those* girls, and girls like *that* don't get back to you on time. And even though I know it's a bad idea, and that by texting her again I'll seem desperate and scare her away, I just can't help myself.

*Text 2—16.20*

*I don't know what I'm looking for. You ever get like that? Where you feel like there's something you want but you don't know what it is. I get like that a lot. I've tried a bunch of things to fix on like being alone and not being alone and drugs and booze and sex and food and television and books and gambling and buying stuff. And I haven't found the combination yet. I know there is a right combination, I just know it, otherwise how does everyone else manage... I tried anti-depressants but they made my head fog. I didn't like that so I stopped. Do you take anti-depressants? I won't judge you if you tell me yes. I like that Lennon line: whatever gets you through the night... I don't know if I've told you that I'm a writer. I tell people I'm a writer but I'm not really. Maybe I could be if I tried but my laziness is holding me back... That's not strictly true. I've been putting some effort in recently but I think the pressure is getting to me. I can't get the good stories in the back of my brain to the front. Does that make sense? If I can sort that out then I will write a great book. I don't care what happens after that. You ever get like that? Not caring. I just want to make sure I do one thing well and famously and then if I fuck everything up after that I won't be too bothered. I'll always be that guy who wrote that great book. Not many people can say that. I also write poetry. It's not any good, or most of it isn't. But I think that's because I need practice. You don't have to write back if you don't want to. This is Huck.*

## Cubby Bear and the hit man

The phone screen is fucking with me. Watching it smile back blankly is screwing with my voices. I leave the phone on the kitchen counter, put on my sweats and head out the door. I walk up Addison. The day is shiny and cold. I play a kid's game: exhaling, pretending to blow smoke. It makes me laugh. And I can't stop. Soon I'm on the floor wheezing, spluttering, making a scene. A passerby passes me by with his kid. "Daddy, why's he laughing?" says the kid. The father grabs his son's hand, pulls him close. He whispers, "Son, that's what'll happen to you if you don't go to school." That's not true and it makes me mad. And I feel *the fury* bubbling up. I did plenty of school. I have all sorts of diplomas telling me I'm this, I'm that, masking me from what I am: one of life's also-rans... I get myself up. I shuffle, I drag, I get myself down the road. And into the Cubby Bear.

The place is dead. Had it been a game day it would've been rammed, and I couldn't have handled it, but as it is, the place is only a quarter full, mostly drunks, serious drinkers, with their drinks and their sadness and their heads down. The only noise comes from TVs blaring sports. I don't mind watching sports. There are no laugh meters in sport, so sport is okay. I order a bourbon and ask the bartender, Lucy, how she's doing. She smiles at me and tells me she has a boyfriend now. She's not saying that out of nowhere. But because I fucked her a couple of years ago. So she's letting me know that she remembers that, but that she's not available anymore. She is polite about it though, not bitchy, so there's no hard feelings there... But just so you know, I wouldn't anyway. See, when I fucked her she was different. She was thirty pounds better off. Now I sit here watching as she waddles between customers, serving drinks, pretending to be okay with things. Of course, she can't be. She's lost her self-worth: what's-the-point is stenciled across her overripe thighs, drips down her heavy legs. I'd understand if she didn't have the face for it but she does. She used to look like Natalie Portman. *That* pretty. It's this job, you know. Late nights, beers, Mexican food after closing—it all adds up. I can see it now. I know what'll happen. She'll end up settling for a guy who's not quite there, and they'll both get comfortable, put on that relationship weight. And suddenly that thirty pounds is fifty and they're "that really fat couple." Then, when they break up, because everybody breaks up, she'll eat lonely buckets of chicken on her grease-stained couch, watching reality television and *Bridget Jones*. Suddenly her fifty pounds over is seventy. And she'll settle again, end up with some morbidly obese depressive, who'll die of a heart attack, leaving her with three screaming kids, all with early onset diabetes, and no health insurance... Jesus. If she could just see what I see. People don't tell you about the upside to bulimia, about the benefits of drug addiction, but I'm telling you, it saves lives. It's just not cool to say it out loud...

Walking back to mine, I see a man I know, used to play cards with—not a friend exactly but a card-playing acquaintance, and I nod my acknowledgment as our distance closes. He is a clipped man, meaning he talks in short, sharp, meaningful phrases. I think because of his time in uniform. Anyway, although I don't particularly care for the man, I do pity him. He is an almost man. Almost handsome, almost rugged. Almost everything. But not quite... He is cellophane wrapped around his girlfriend. Who is *not* almost anything. She is stunning, and she knows it too. It's hard being in his shoes. Like I say, I feel sorry for him. Being the lesser of the two, you have more to lose. And I know he's constantly holding his breath, waiting for *the talk*. That's why I don't go for tens. I am an eight, which is great if you figure an average is five. I can handle nines and not be too nervy. But stick me with a ten and I'm a shivering wreck of a man unable to hold an erection even with the wind in my corner. But this guy, he's a six, maybe a six and a pinch, and he's with a solid nine. There's no way a three-point differential can work—not without incentive... Right as they're approaching he suddenly yanks her into the middle of the road and crosses over, turning back and waving apologetically to me as if he forgot he had to do something. I wave back. I get his pain. He sees I'm an eight and he's just being smart. She looks back and eye-fucks me hard. Yeah, he did the right thing... I smile. I just got validated by a nine. An hour ago I was getting rejected by a thirty-pound-over waitress I wasn't even trying to fuck. Yeah, things are looking up... The walk down Addison is not a long one, technically, but I have old limbs, old aches, a rundown system. Recently I've found getting in and out of taxis a struggle. I make those getting out sighs reserved for old people. Between me and you, I don't have a lot of time left...

*Who's that guy? Who's that guy?* I get a cold sweat, a bones chill. I know I've seen that man before. I saw him outside Cubby Bear as I entered. Saw him looking at me, looking at me *without* looking at me—very professional and I almost didn't spot it. But I did. But then I went inside and got sidetracked by drink and other thoughts.

And convinced myself it was just one of my paranoids... *Who's he with?* It could be Cali. She's not above hiring someone to follow me around, make sure I'm not seeing to someone behind her back. Or worse. It could be Jimmy. Jesus, if he knew. Christ, I'd be dead. I take a closer look, but without looking, like he's doing to me. I try to spot a concealed bulge. If Jimmy knows, and I'm not saying he does, but *if* he does he knows the right people—and these could be my last moments. Fuck. Christ... I become a shopper. I go into places. I buy things. I come out of one store and walk into the next. That's the way you lose a tail. You keep moving in and out, in and out. I cross the street. I cross back. I make unexpected movements... I don't see him. I've lost my man... I walk down Addison, a little easier, and find a bum begging for change. They are everywhere in America. People with not enough stuff. With not *nearly* enough. "Here," I say, placing my cover in front of him. He gets gum, water, a Cubs cap, a slice. He doesn't say thank you. He just stares through me. And I think about Red. And I get sad.

I reach my building, head on swivel, eyes glued for the tail, shaking with the adrenaline of an almost death. *Fuck.* I open the door and ride the elevator to six...

A familiar silhouette greets me, gathers in the darkness against my door, sending a jolt of fear into my spine, into the heart of my main nerves. I can see her teeth shine, as they light up the blackness, her eyes dance, can almost *feel* her badness brush up against me.

The noose tightens. I can hear it, hear the karma grip: *You're going to get yours. I'm coming for you, hard.*

"Key."

She owns me; and I give her the key, and we go inside.

"We're going to play rape."

So we do. Because she says so. Because she owns me like I said. Choking games, forced sex. She's into some heavy stuff. When it's over, I look at her neck.

"Jesus." She must have been close to the safety word—she picked the word "fix." "Look at your neck."

"Don't be such a girl. I liked it."

"Cali?"

"Yes?"

"This has to be the last time."

"Why?"

"Jimmy will kill me, is why."

She laughs.

"You're always so melodramatic, Huck. You know Jimmy doesn't leave his apartment. Not unless he's reloading. He's a lot more careful since the robbery, you know."

She gives me the wink.

When she's done with me, she gets up, dresses, tells me to expect her when she comes, then leaves.

*I don't want to die.* I didn't realize that until she came back into town, in the process putting her hands around my neck. The bathtub was my father, was just a sadness, not anything real... And I know that now. And I don't want to die.

# Chapter 13

Rewind six months

She wore skimpy outfits. Whenever I'd come over she'd be draped across his couch, more naked than not. With a pile of bulimic magazines on the coffee table, a phallic joint resting between her painted lips. Her legs. I loved her legs the most. Long and tan and packaged in ultra-high cut-offs... She does everything well and for maximum effect. Like all hot messes, she breathes the attention. She gets off on watching guys' eyes pop... She'd always smile at me, say hi, and I'd get hard and say hi back. But this was Jimmy's girl. And with him being homicidally violent, viciously volatile, I kept our fuck sessions strictly in my head, masturbating furiously whenever I got home from a Jimmy run... She knew I liked her though. Just by how much effort I put into acting like I didn't...

One day I'm over when Jimmy gets a call. There is lots of swearing, cursing, shouting. Jimmy throws things. And I don't like that, and I get nervous.

"What's the matter with you?"

"Nothing, Jimmy."

"Look," he says, "I need to do a run. You keep an eye on her for me?"

He points to Cali, she smiles at me, and I get anxious.

"I don't know, man," I say. "I have to be—"

"Shouldn't be more than an hour. I just can't leave her here on her own. You can't trust women, man," he says—and he says it loud and right in front of her and it feels awkward—"they're all schemers."

"That's right," she says, "you can't."

Then they laugh, him and her. I don't laugh. I don't like conflict.

"I can't, Jimmy. I have to go return some videotapes."

"You're doing it, kid," he says, "and that's that."

And I don't like friction. So I do him the favor.

... The door closes and she wastes no time steaming me up.

"Pass me the lotion."

I pass her the lotion.

"Don't get the wrong idea," she says. "I just have to moisturize to keep my legs right."

"I won't get the wrong idea," I say.

I watch as she stretches her legs out, coats her fingers in cream, rubs her hands into her leg tissue. She does it slow, *real* slow. She keeps eye contact with me the whole time. She smiles. She pouts her lips. She keeps repeating. More lotion on her fingers, more rubbing, smiling, eye contact... I almost lose my shit, rip off her clothes, take her actions as consent. But I don't give myself the green light. The thought of Jimmy chopping me up, blending me into sausage meat, stops me. Instead I do the honorable thing: I go to the toilet. But then karma deals me my usual hand... It turns out there's something wrong with the lock and California walks in as I'm closing in. I freeze. I expect her to scream or run or call me a dirty son of a bitch, but I don't get any of that. Instead, like an old pro, she eases her panties aside and straddles me. And it's good. And it's very, very good. And seconds later I'm finishing inside...

I couldn't prove she'd robbed Jimmy. But I knew she had. Mention it and her eyes became *too* wry, her frown *too* smug. Jimmy, of course, was too love-drunk to notice. As she knew he would be. *Clever girl...* So when she told me she required five thousand dollars to leave town, I gave it her even though I knew she didn't need it. Five thousand dollars, I thought, was a very fair price to bury my slip from Jimmy...


On the run

I hear heavy-handed knocking. A barrage of bone on wood. I consider telling her to go away, but I know California, know she'll make a scene, get the neighbors involved, possibly the police. So I yell that I'm coming. Climb off the couch and open the door...

And stare. In horror. *Jimmy.* I look down at his hands. For weapons. *No weapons.* He pushes past, pulls me in, closes the door...

Fast-thinking, bad information and misdirection keep me alive. I handle a handful of California questions, obviously admitting nothing, other than my innocence...

In the end, Jimmy leaves *without* cutting my throat. He tells me not to go anywhere. I give him my best smile and assure him I'll be staying put...

Five minutes after Jimmy departs, I am, of course, outside my apartment, frantically flagging down my escape. In the cab, paranoia slides me down my seat. And when I am low enough that I am sure no one can see me, I tell the driver to drive me to The Drake. I swear an oath to the driver that I will stay at the hotel indefinitely. He says I must be rich. I hand him a hundred dollars.

## The Drake Hotel—the first twelve days

A middle-aged couple, her draped in jewels, him draped in her, check in ahead of me. Apart from the three of us the lobby is empty. This is the skinny season, there are cutbacks all round.

When they're done, they grab their room cards, and turn, and we're two feet apart, all three of us staring. The woman visibly withdraws. "Jesus," she says. "What?" I snap. "Can I help you?" says the man, stepping in front of his girl. I smile. He thinks he's doing the brave thing, the chivalrous play. He doesn't know I can't fight, that I only had one lucky punch in me, and it's already been used. He looks me up and down, and grimaces. I keep my smile on. "You've got the wrong idea, man. I'm an actor," I tell him. "I like to go method." He lets out his relief. I extend my hand and he shakes it. "RDJ," I say. "Henry." He points to the woman. "And this is Georgiana." One more round of pleasantries—weather talk—then they turn the corner for the elevator, and I step forward. A pleasant smile greets me.

"Can I help you, sir?"

I smile back, but don't say anything, just thrust my card at the man in uniform.

"Sir?"

"Yes?"

"How can I help you?"

"Oh, right," I say, "a room please."

"What would you like, we've got—"

"I'd like a suite if you have one," I say. "Any suite will do."

"Yes, sir, Mr. Downey Jr."

I grimace, glance left and right, and put my fingers to my lips.

"I'd rather we keep this visit quiet," I say. "Just need some down time. You understand."

"Discretion. Yes, sir. Sorry, sir."

I smile.

"That's cool, man. See you around."

A boy, a young man, a teenager, shows me to my room. He doesn't carry my bags because I don't have any. I grabbed my laptop, hugged up my book-maker, nothing else. I left my apartment in a rush, in a daze, in a frightened flurry, and I'll have to buy clothes, comfortable clothes, clothes for writing, writer's clothes. And shoes. I am wearing slippers and I'll have to buy shoes of some sort, probably sneakers, writers wear sneakers... When we get to the room I tip the boy fifty, a movie star tip, a Robert Downey Jr. thank-you. For the rest of my stay, for however long that may be, my aim is to convince the staff that I'm *the* Robert Downey Jr. It shouldn't be too hard. He's had periods of hardness—trouble with booze, a dance with drugs—plus I look like him, or so I've been told. No, it shouldn't be too hard. Normal folk want to meet famous people—so they can have *that story* to tell. Their hope will tell their eyes to tell their brains that I'm the real deal. The boy nods, a tight nod, takes the money, turns and leaves. I head straight to the mini bar and pour out the contents onto the bed. Nothing looks appealing to me. And I put it all back.

I take a long shower, using all the little bottles. No matter what it is, I pour it all together—the shampoo, conditioner, bubble bath, the lot—all into a big puddle in my hands, and rub it all over. I feel gooey, and luxurious. I rinse off then dress myself in a toweled robe that says I've made it. I feel silly-rich. The soft, thick toweling, the slippers that kiss my toes, tell my brain that I'm worth a hundred million dollars. Is this what it feels like to have that kind of money, *real* money, unspendable riches?

I call downstairs and tell them I'll need a bottle of five-hundred-dollar scotch, two cheeseburgers, two fries, and a milkshake. They ask me what scotch. I tell them I don't care, just make sure it's five hundred dollars. They tell me ten minutes. That's what I love about places like this. You can be completely unreasonable and no one bats an eyelid. If I make it big I want to live here. People do that, you know. Fall in love with things like room service and pay-per-view, and hide away forever (or until the money runs out).

The food comes. I time it too. It takes eight minutes for two perfectly cooked cheeseburgers, hot fries, the scotch and the milkshake to arrive. Since my first tip was fifty, they'll know me as a fifty-dollar man. Therefore anyone getting less will think he's done something wrong and, if they're anything like me, they'll have a word with a friend, a kitchen hand, and suddenly I'm getting spit in my food. Even if I check and can't see it, I'll know it's there, and I'll never be able to eat, and I'll starve to death. I dole out another fifty-dollar tip.

The milkshake is the best I've ever had—and I've had hundreds. Same with the fries. They do them crispy, like the old McDonald's fries before over-salting was boardroomed out. The burgers, too, are pretty outstanding. They needed more cheese, and I ordered more cheese, and they brought me more cheese, and another fifty dollar tip... I have to throw up after the meal. Maybe I went too fast, or it was too rich, or I'm just dying, but I spend some time hovering over the toilet bowl, my eyes watering, until everything is out... When I'm done I take a Coke from the mini-bar and drain it. Coke is always the best cure for most anything. I drain another and feel better. I put on a movie, sit back on the bed, relax, and swig scotch from the bottle, as I watch. Girl meets guy, guy notices girl, girl ignores guy, then magically everyone notices everyone, and they end up happily together... everything has a bow on it, no one ends up losing out, the end... The scotch is good but disappointing. I thought that over a certain price scotch would stop tasting like scotch. But it doesn't.

When I'm good and oiled I start typing. *Title*. I'm calling the book "Me." A simple, original title, that'll get other, lesser writers, cutting themselves for not nailing it down first. It pushes the curious button all the way to the checkout line. A great start, I am immensely proud. **_Chapter 1_**. I bold, italicize and wait... Anyone can write a book. To do it well takes patience. See, if you get nervous, dive head first into the opening scene, you'll come out desperate. Your words will be strained, your story line torced. And they'll feel it, those page turners, and they'll change the fucking channel. You've got a page, two pages tops, and if you haven't hooked them by then, well... you're fucked... That's why I can sit here now—sipping five-hundred-dollar swill—with nothing but the title, and no idea of a story, and smile. Because I know what mistakes _not_ to make. I'm way ahead of the field. Me, I'm practically at the finish line... Pleased with myself, I close my computer and take a bath. I've used up all the complimentary soap products so I call down and order a basket of "bubble stuff" along with champagne and strawberries, and dental floss for the seeds.

On lockdown twelve days and not a word yet. No spark, no kick-start to the engine. Just room service and pay-per-view and bubble baths and prostitutes... I was in the bar on my second night, taking a break from my room, when a beautiful girl asked me to buy her a drink. Cut to an hour later and we're transacting up in my suite. She stayed the night, an unnecessary extravagance, what with me having faulty wiring. I didn't know how these things worked, well you don't until you do, do you? That me not dismissing her equated to continued business. So, when I woke up, still half-cut, I got some sobering news, in the form of a verbal invoice for services almost rendered. I didn't have the three thousand on my person, and since I couldn't charge this to the room, we had to take an uncomfortable walk with her and her minder to a nearby cash point. "Next time yous have moneys readies, yes?" he said, in thick, impatient, imported tones. "Yes," I replied, "I offer my sincerest, Yohan. Furthermore, I do hope this doesn't impact negatively on our friendship, yes?" Luckily my sarcastic slant went wide of target, so instead of slapping me around for my rapier wit he handed me a business card. "You call this number, tell type need, we do price, and deliver, yes?" I had no intention of calling the number, not at those prices, but an intent in the morning is tested in the lonely hours, and I have dialed five times since... By and large though I've been keeping to myself, often spending the afternoons staring at the keyboard, fingers over keys, ready... There have been some distractions. Like the maids wanting to clean my room. I let them at it the first two days, but then afterward I had to throw the RDJ around. I called down and spoke to the manager and said that I couldn't be disturbed, that I needed solitude. "For the role," I said. He was very understanding. People always are, given the right wrong information... And my phone. My phone was giving me grief. Lots of calls from Cali and Jimmy, lots of angry texts, violent messages. So I keep it off. Occasionally I switch it on to see if Stella has called, but nothing.


Stella and me, and the screenplay

(makes three)

This is my thirteenth day. I have reached saturation point with milkshakes and burgers, and although I still throw up most of what I eat I retain enough to start seeing a little meat coming back to me. I can still see the ribs, but they are not as pronounced and I have a flat stomach now instead of a crescent coming in... I switch on my phone again. I have a text from Stella.

*Been mad busy, kiddo. Need a drink though. Join me.*

I write back.

*Join me. I'm at The Drake. I've been holed up here writing, or trying to write.*

I don't hear anything back, so I text her again, this time with a dirty joke and my room number. I tell her I'll be here for the foreseeable, that she can come by whenever she wants. Then I drink some more, get nervous about not writing, write two different versions of opening paragraphs. But they both stink. Reinforcing my belief that you can't force these things, that magic takes time. I pass out... There is knocking at my door. Maybe I ordered room service before I blacked out. "Who is it?" I yell. "Room service," comes back the reply in short, clipped, accented English. I tie up my robe. I sigh. I've been living in it since I got here; it is dirty and stained and lacks the fluffy luxury of before. I open the door. It is not a tray but grinning that greets me. "You beautiful son of a bitch! We've got lots to talk about, but first I need a drink like you wouldn't believe. Come on." And with that she pushes past me, closes the door, presses her lips onto mine, her tongue inviting me to play. "You taste like scotch. I'd kill for some scotch. And sex. I need sex like a son of a bitch." Things are looking up for old Huck. Karma, perhaps, is taking a long overdue nap... In the afterglow of the afterward, we lie there. It is awkward like it always is following that first time.

"You look fucking horrendous," she says, holding up the miniatures, silently mouthing the labels. She passes me one. "What have you been up to?"

"Writing. I've been here two weeks." I take the miniature down. "You're the first person I've seen."

"Really?" she says. "Writing what?"

"Nothing so far," I say. "It's a process."

"How incredibly full of shit."

"Excuse me?"

"I've dated writers that talk like that. And it's bull. If you want to write, you know what the secret is?"

"I'm all ears."

"Writing. To be a writer you have to write."

She must have Rumi on speed dial.

"Come on." She gets up and hoists me to my feet then propels me like a rag doll through the bathroom door. "Take a shower—you stink, by the way—then let's go to the bar and get hammered."

I do not protest. Writing is hard; drinking is easy; getting drunk with Stella is fun. I take a shower: short, cold, perfunctory.

We go down for drinks. At the entrance to the bar we encounter a group of young, tanned, winner-type men, all wearing rugby jerseys, talking in loud, Australian swagger.

Stella glides past them, pulling my aching limbs along in her slipstream. Silence erupts as seven sets of super-white perfect teeth emerge to greet us. As I knew it would, a voice booms toward us, almost bowling me over. "Tell me you're not with him?" Without missing a beat she informs the hoard that I am anatomically gifted, and that perhaps their need to hide in packs indicates an unfortunate lacking in packing. They don't have a comeback for that, and I laugh, and we go to a table in the middle and sit down. I want somewhere dark and in the back, but Stella insists on being *involved*, so we end sitting sandwiched between conversations.

"You ever play the guessing game?"

"What's that?"

"Okay," she says, "so what we do is pick someone and make up a bio. It's fun."

She points to a woman sat on her own.

"Go on," she says, "you try first."

"I'm really not in the mood, Stella. Let's just drink."

Stella lets out an exasperated sigh.

"Look, it's none of my business but..."

"Yes?"

"Shouldn't you be *trying* to work on your imagination?"

"And why's that?"

"Because you're a writer."

She makes a good point. And I tell her that too. And she stops pouting. We go around the room, picking people, taking it in turns to assassinate their characters, making wild leaping judgments and baseless assessments. It is fun being judge and jury, and the drinks flow, and the time passes. The only low point comes when Stella excuses herself to take a work call. I scan the room, my eye catching hopelessness: a young girl folding herself into the mannerisms of her mother. I see the necessary cycle: who she will become, who her children will become—and hate. And it's all so terribly sad. So horrifically inevitable.

... I am in that place—that small space of time when I can still remember my dreams. I curtain-off from reality and start playing it back:

*I am a poker player. I sit at the final table of the World Series, Johnny Chan to my right, Doyle Brunson to my left, I have the high stack, no cards but I'm reading the game, the men, the man, perfectly. Brunson shakes his head, pays me a compliment, says I'm a natural. Doyle Brunson, Johnny Fucking Chan...*

*I am a sprinter, Olympic finals, middle lane, hundred meters. I break the world record, smash it, go under nine seconds, set a record that will never be beaten, says the commentator. I destroy the field, the stadium goes silent, deadly silent, then erupts in pandemonium. Usain Bolt comes over to me, tells me I'm the best that'll ever be. Usain fucking Bolt.*

*I am a big-time movie actor. I walk down the street, women swoon, men stare bullets. I make a movie, with my own money, small indie flick. I do it my way, no compromises, no Hollywood, no polling. I direct. I act. I win Academies for both. I stick Jolie in as the lead girl and steal her away from Pitt. I am that cool, I can take a woman from Pitt. Brad fucking Pitt.*

*I am a singer-songwriter. I make music. My music. I refuse to sign to a label, get tied to a contract. I put everything out on my own label.* Rolling

Stone *writes an article about me. They call it: Reintroducing Kurt Cobain. Kurt fucking Cobain.*

"Hey get up. Let's get to it."

"Five more minutes."

"No. Get up now."

"Sounds good."

I graze my finger up her thigh, she doesn't slap me. Then higher and higher. And we're at it again. I keep waiting for it to stop working, for it to fall off, but for some reason the drink isn't calling the shots. Although I don't know why. Probably still karma taking her nap...

"Men. I swear," she laughs, "you could be fucking a girl and still think you weren't getting enough."

"True."

"You were a scream last night."

"Is that good?"

"Yes."

"What happened?"

"We batted around a few screenplay ideas."

"Really?"

"Yes."

"But I'm writing a book."

"How much of it have you written?"

I ignore the question.

"So we're writing a screenplay?"

# Chapter 14

Exiting The Drake, entering the motel

Four days after Stella's arrival—a time of trying to write and writing nothing, of moving rooms and causing havoc—a badly timed phone call necessitates our hasty exit. The manager, who takes personal pleasure in checking us out, does not hide his happiness at news of our departure. We have not been model guests. Along with room rental and food and beverage charges, a large damages fee has been viciously attached. Stella, certain we're being taken for a ride, wants to stick around, beat the figure down to a more reasonable sum—but I'm keen on keeping my pulse so agree to pay in full.

We're in the cab now... Half an hour ago I'd been neck-deep in bubbles and gin, and having a grand old time, when the phone—which, admittedly, I'd quite carelessly forgotten to switch off—rang. Stella, being a typically curious girl, answered, and had a long and informative conversation with Jimmy the Jew—giving him my current location and, rather unfortunately, graphic details of our sexual exploits. Which is the *why* we had to leave. See—and maybe I should have told you this before—but Jimmy had always assumed I was gay. I suspect it has something to do with me living in Boystown, being, when I so choose, an impeccable dresser, and failing to understand football's rules and regulations. Misinformation that no doubt saved my life the day he came round to mine, hot on the tail of California. He—whose agoraphobia is apparently not as severe as I had been comforted to believe—had been tailing her, convinced, quite correctly, that she was screwing around. "I know it's not you, boy. No, just to look at you I know you like the cock. Hell, I caught you checking me out, remember? Still, you're going to have to tell me what she was doing here, sport." So, over drinks, that's exactly what I did. Playing the old switcheroo. I explained that she was convinced *he* was fucking around on *her*. "She doesn't blame you though, Jimmy. Says it's her fault for walking out before. Anyway, now she wants me to spy on you, on account of me and you being tight." When he left my apartment, an hour or so later, we'd made a deal. I promised that I'd be his eyes and ears. Whatever she told me, I'd tell him. And he wanted regular reports. "Let her come here, but after she leaves, tail her, find out where she goes, who she sees. And Huck—don't fuck it up." After he left, it took me all of five minutes to decide it was only a matter of time before he had my number. (Cali has a hot head, loose tongue, bad judgment. Or he might even catch us in the act.) I had no choice. I had to go on the run... Which is how I ended up at The Drake—where everything was going fine *until* the phone call... *Jesus*, Jimmy will kill me when he sees me. He'll grind my bones to make his bread...

"This is a good thing," she says. "Perfect, in fact."

"How'd you figure that?"

"Thing about it. Writers are *supposed* to be desperate."

"*Okay.*"

"Otherwise the work is beige."

"I agree."

"So no *wonder* we couldn't produce. We were too busy living it up."

"Yeah, that's probably why. So what do we do about it?"

"We need to get a room in some downtrodden, Aids-infested, crack den of a motel..."

... She tells the driver to take us to the worst motel he knows. He says he knows some pretty bad motels and we wouldn't do well there. But Stella gets how Stella gets and after a few minutes of arguing and an extra forty dollars he agrees to take us there.

When we pull up, he gets into it with Stella. Despite the forty, and the promise of more, he refuses to get out of the cab and help us with our luggage. "There's a bad element here, its not for me," he says. We get out, drag ourselves, our luggage, over to a lazy-eyed, twitchy, Korean girl behind a thick glass plate. Despite it being the only obvious requirement, she appears to speak no American, none whatsoever. Ten minutes of hand gestures, and we find ourselves in a room that stinks of piss and sweat and sex and sick. I want to open a window but the windows are screwed shut. I light a cigarette to clean the air and watch as Stella jumps up and down on the bed, squealing with delight. She is happy, then very happy, then the springs break, and the bed collapses. She insists we christen the room. Lying on my back, on the floor, her straddling me, it feels like I'm sharing a room with a thousand hookers. It gets me excited and hard and I finish in record time.

## Shelonda

We are a long way from *good* Chicago. We are in the land of the urban hustler. The marketing out here is aggressive, violent, often homicidal. But we are drunks, and drunks need alcohol, so I tell Stella to stay put and head out in search of a liquor store. *Avoid eye contact, keep your head down, your mouth shut, your feet moving...* I am told to buy crack. I say nothing. I am offered heroin. I say nothing. I am offered a child. To fuck. I stand still. The fury stands me still. The pimp pushes his merchandise forward, and tells her to talk... And her words are bullets. And my heart breaks... "My name is Shelonda," she says. "I am thirteen. I will fuck you, suck you, take it in the ass..." She quotes me a list of prices for the things I can do, the ways she can please me. The list is long and sick and wrong and I get *the fury* and I look at the pimp, look at how big he is, how street, and tough, and I despise myself for how I cannot fight, for how worthless, for how not a man, I am...

When I don't say anything to the girl, the pimp steps forward.

"Well? What do you want?"

I don't say anything.

"You a fag?"

*The fury draws a knife from my pocket, sticks him in the face, in the cheek, puts it right through... then, when he's spitting blood, and doubled over, I stick it to him in the side of the neck... and again and again, and the head and the chest and the ears and the brain... and it's raining blood... and his eyes are with me... and the floor is slippery with his life... and his eyes are gone... they are gone and he is gone and she is smiling and she is free and I have freed her and I have...*

"Hey. I'm *fucking* talking to you..."

I don't say anything.

"What's the matter? You too good for Shelonda?"

I don't say anything.

"She mine... You too good for me, boy, huh, that it?"

I don't say anything.

"Look at her, she's *young*, she's tight..."

I don't say anything... he raises his hand, like he's going to hit me... I brace myself... But he punches her instead. Punches her like she's a man—closed fist, and full force—in the stomach, though, because it's better for business... She falls to the floor. And I watch her fall. And cough. And the tears come down. And her eyes meet mine, saying please, saying help, and I look away... look away and pretend like it's a TV show. Otherwise it would be too much, the guilt, the shitty feeling of somehow my fault... And I don't remember the rest. I know he keeps talking to me, keeps taunting, and I don't say anything, and I expect him to hit me, but he doesn't... I only remember the end credits: of him grabbing her, turning her wrist, taking her away, away for a lesson. And I watch... I watch and do nothing and he drags her away...

Weeks come and go. We sit, drink, reload at the store. We never leave the room, only for supplies. I make the walk. I keep my wallet in the room, the necessary money in my sock. No watch, rings, jewelry, no reasons to target. I am white, yes, but I look poor white, not bullseye white, payday white. I keep an eye open for Shelonda. I see her pimp with other girls—young girls, *very* young, younger than Shelonda even—and I wish he would die, bite a bullet, suck it down, down his throat, let it rip through his chest, through the steel, the armory, into his double-black heart. He is soulless, an animal. He is godless. And I wish he would die.

We do not work. At first we pretend like we're going to start, but after a few days the talk of tomorrow, of beginning tomorrow, stops, and we just sit and drink and drink.

And the sex... After a while we do not fuck. We become drunks in the rhythm of booze—sex becomes an afterthought, a nothing, a distraction. My blood's not flowing right, anyway. Making me not a man at all. And I drink on that.

All we do is drink and talk. Until the talking goes. And we sit in silence, in sickness, day and night, day and night. In a cramped, deprived hole we huddle together, drinking, drinking alone, not together. Drunks drink alone, not together.

... Then one day, it's over. Stella wakes me up and tells me we have to leave. So we leave. We walk out onto the street, walk three blocks to a main street, a safe street, hail a cab, get in and go. I ask the driver the date, and he tells it me. We've been at the motel five weeks.

# Chapter 15

Sideboard sickness

Stella turns to me, grabs my arm, squeezes.
"Huck...?"
"Yeah?"
"I'm going back to my apartment."
"Okay."
"So... It's a nice place..."
"Okay."
"... plenty of room."
"Okay."
"Stop saying 'okay,' okay?"
"Sure."
She takes her hand off of my arm, rests it on my lap. There is a long pause. It feels weird.
"You need me to say it, don't you?"
"Say what?"
"It's cruel of you. But alright..."
"Stella...?"
"Yeah?"
"I really don't know what you're talking about."
"Christ, I'm saying you can move in."

"Right."

"Not like *permanently* or anything—just until we've finished the script."

"Right."

"Of course, the first thing we need to do is start writing."

"Right."

"I can't believe we haven't gotten around to that yet."

"Yes. I too am surprised."

She's been stroking my thigh, not in a sexual way, you understand, no—just in a nice, friendly, fuzzy-warm way. She immediately stops.

"You mocking me?"

"Okay."

She laughs, punches me on the arm, on the funny bone. I get knee-jerk tears, that well up and fall. She sees.

"You crying?"

I ignore the question, turn for a second, wipe away the evidence.

"Of course not," I say. "Listen, I have to drop by my place, sort some things out. But I'll come over when I'm done. Okay?"

She punches me on the arm.

"And once you're done you'll come over?"

"Yes."

"And we'll write the screenplay?"

"Yes."

"Promise?"
"Promise."

This is a lie, of course. I have long since accepted that we are not writing a screenplay. But are just two drunks, drinking, lying to each other, lying next to each other. And that's fine with me. I hate the loneliness, and she stops the loneliness, and pretending to write is a small price to pay, to have that relieved.

The cab drops me outside my apartment. I watch the cab shuffle off, a little out of its lane, and swerving some, albeit at a slow speed. The driver was drinking and maybe a little drunk. He wasn't stupid, though—he hid it in a Coke cup. But I could tell. I know these things. Still, it's not ideal, and I hope Stella makes it back okay. And that the driver makes it back okay. Drunks are victims too, you know. It's a disease. A terrible disease with a terrible death count. And I hope everyone gets home safe.

I do not go up to my apartment. I miss Red. I don't know why. It might be spending all this time with a girl, it might be other things. I can't really put my finger on it. But I know that I miss him, and I wonder, as I stand here, right now, outside my apartment, if he misses me... I poke my head around the side of the building, down the alleyway, half expecting to see my old friend... He is not there. No one is. It is empty...

Another cab takes me to the financial district. It is almost eight in the evening. We arrive, I pay, I get out, I start patrolling the streets. I am here because Ed sleeps here. If Red is still around I expect him to be with Ed. They are close, from what Red told me, and if he's not trying to track down his family, if he's not with his family, if he's not dead, I expect him to be with Ed... I plow the roads, looking. Up and down. Across. Up and down... I don't know how long I do it for. But it's a long time. And when my legs get too tired and I start to wheeze and feel faint, I sit down and have a rest and a drink... And before I know it, it's two in the morning and the bars are closing and all the friends I've made have gone home. And I'm too drunk. And I can't see straight. And I have a hard time hailing a cab...

When I get back to mine, I pass out. I lose consciousness in the hallway. I do not make it into bed. I throw up. All over the sideboard that my father gave me. I try to clean it up. I cry as I try to get it all. But everything goes black...

When I wake up I have sick down the side of my face, in a towel in my hand, down my neck, in my hair. The sick is all over. Covering, smothering the sideboard. And my father is watching. And I cry. I cry harder than after the funeral, than at the funeral, than the crying I did for when my mother left—in my room on my own, so my father couldn't hear. I cry real hard. And my father is watching. And my mother is not. Not watching. Not caring about me. And I keep on crying.


Party of five

The day after the sideboard sickness, I continued looking for Red. I trolled the streets again. I stopped homeless people. I asked them about Red. I described him, in detail, but no one helped I got strange looks, weary looks, no language, just grunts and cold shoulders... I gave up, like I always do, after a good idea gets too hard on the follow-through... And I went back to my neighborhood, back to Wrigley, but not to my apartment, but out, looking for a deep drunk, and after, an obliteration...

I remember everything. Clear as crystal. Which is strange for a heavy drunk, but not unheard of. I remember making enemies. I remember the enemies I made. Big ones, tall ones, quiet ones, mean ones. One in particular, after I made my impression on him, took pleasure in making his impression on me...

I picked him because he was too tough—for me, for an army of me—and I knew that he should be the one, to do the work... So I went over. To the table where he sat, in the middle of a crowded bar, alone, nursing his drink, with dead eyes, half-circling, scanning for prey.

*I stand over him. The air is sucked out of the room. He looks up. I look down. I smile. I pick up his drink, drain the glass, grin, turn the glass on its head, crash it down on the table, smashing glass, shards everywhere...*

That's what I did. Because I wanted it that night. I wanted the oblivion... "Come on," I said, loud enough for the dead—my dead, and the general dead—to hear, "if you're serious about your seriousness, show me what you've got. Outside now."

... A vicious left, a crunching right, combination punches, elbows, knees, his head smashing into my nose, making my eyes bleed, my ears ring... The more that came down, the closer I felt to nothing, the less it hurt, the less it hurt being me. So I kept pushing him. From on the floor, vision gone, body battered, I kept shouting, calling him a coward, a pedophile, a rapist. I wanted it to be forever—*so I kept pushing* —for the pain to be removed forever—for this healing to never stop.

But then it stopped... *I'm being pulled to my feet. And then blackness...*

I wake up, in bed. My body sore, my head sore, no bones broken, although I don't know how. Red and Ed. They are here. With me. In my apartment. And I don't know how. I ask them to tell me what happened... I want to hear a story about them coming over and beating up on a guy that beat up on me, that they did that, put themselves on the line, for me, like that. But my ears get different, get less... get that a crowd was gathered, that they—Ed and Red—gathered to, that they saw me in the middle, that they pulled me to my feet, that they put me in a cab, took me home...

I tell Red that I've missed him. Ed asks me if I've missed him too. I tell him no that I haven't, and he asks me why not. And I tell him it's because I don't like him. "Not even a little?" he asks. "Not even a little," I say. He goes quiet, then grins, then laughs and tells me that he didn't like me either. "Except, now I like you. Now we're going to be good friends." I tell him I disagree. He doesn't get angry, like I expect, he just says he's sure of it, and that I should trust him. I don't trust him, but I'm bruised up pretty bad so I let it go... I ask Red if he would like to move in. He tells me he will, but only if Ed can stay too. So I tell him okay. I'm bruised up pretty bad, so I tell him okay...

I stay in bed. Until the afternoon. When there is knocking at my door. I climb out of bed. My whole body hurts. Walking hurts, breathing hurts, time hurts. I answer the door. Stella is at the door. She tries to get angry for a minute—I was supposed to come over—but she sees the state of me, and cuts into her opening.

"Holy shit! What happened to you?"
"Nothing."
"Bullshit, nothing. Holy shit..."

"I'm fine."

"Huck. What happened?"

"I was minding my own business. Having a quiet drink. But this guy, this fucking guy, just wouldn't stop fucking with me so I fucked with him back."

"Is he hurt pretty bad?"

"No. He's fine."

"Really?"

"Yeah. Turns out he's a pretty good fighter."

"What did the guy do to you?"

"It wasn't what he did to me exactly. It was more... I could tell what he had done to other people, and I wasn't standing for it."

"Listen..."

"I don't think I will. Sorry. Now—you can either come in or not come in. Either is fine with me. Just don't give me any shit."

So there we are, all on my bed: me, Stella, Ed and Red, all getting thoroughly drunk. When there is knocking at my door. I try to get to my feet but my body is blown up something rotten, and my legs won't work, and my arms won't work. So I ask someone to get the door... Jimmy is here. At the door. Any other time and I'd be shit scared to see him, but after last night, I don't give too much of a damn if he stabs me or shoots me or chokes me to death. So I stand there. And stare him down. And he stands there. And stares me down. And that goes on for a while.

"California," he says, "she left me."

"Okay."

"I thought she might be here."

"Okay."

"But she's not. Right?"

"Right."

"Only I thought it could have been you she was fucking…"

"Okay."

"After I discovered you weren't gay. And I followed her here. And you fled your place. And you stopped picking up my calls. And she left me. You add all that together and you have to be fucking her."

"Okay."

"But she isn't here."

"That's right, Jimmy. She isn't here."

"Then she wasn't fucking you."

"Okay."

"Sorry, Huck."

"Okay."

"For accusing you. That was fucked up."

"Okay."

And that's how it became the five of us… I *wanted* Red to stay, and Ed came with Red. Then Stella came over. And I didn't care if she stayed or didn't stay, but she ended up staying, because she's lonely like that. Then Jimmy came over. And pretty much had a break down in front of the four of us.

Said he was seriously depressed after California left him. That he needed somewhere to crash, because he couldn't be on his own. That being in his apartment all day, smoking dope, lifting weights, was really screwing with his head. And I felt weird about turning him away, especially since I suspected that I could've been a better friend. So when he asked me, I said he could crash. For a little while at least.

# Chapter 16

### Rolling over

I do dishes. Red, Ed, Stella do dishes... Jimmy does not do dishes. Jimmy eats off the same plate. Washes the same plate with his tongue first, then his saliva-soaked fingers, then his tongue again, then finally with a splash from the tap. Then he puts it away. Away from the other plates, atop the fridge. Along with a knife and fork, cleaning the same as the plate. "I don't create dish mess," he says, "I don't *un*create dish mess. I am a self-contained unit. I am an island."

I go to the store for liquor. I go to the liquor store, to the 7-Eleven down the block, or the discount place, four blocks down. I take Stella when I go. Either I go with Stella. Or Red goes with Ed. When Red goes with Ed, I give Red—I still don't trust Ed—the money. He comes back with liquor and beer and a receipt and the correct change. He doesn't rip me off. He doesn't even try. And I bet Ed would try, which is why I never give him the money... Jimmy does not do drink runs. "I am not an alcoholic," he says. "I could take it or leave it. Not like you guys." He waves his fingers at us, accusing. "You guys are fucked up. You need to get your acts together." He pauses to roll a joint. "You need to stop drinking. That's what you need. Me, I can take a drink or not take a drink and it doesn't much matter to me. So I don't go to the store. Because I don't *need* to go to the store." He still drinks our drinks though. He still takes our medicine. And we don't say it, but we think it, think we don't like it. Because we are drunks. And drunks need drinks. And he's stealing our medicine. And right in front of us. Right in front of our thirsty eyes.

I do not sleep in my bed. I used to sleep in my bed, on the left, Stella on the right. Red on the couch, Ed on the couch, Jimmy on the reclining chair (one of those chairs that goes back all the way flat, that's better than some beds). But I do not sleep in my bed. Not anymore. Not most nights anyway. I sleep in my bed two nights out of five. Forty percent of the time. Less than half the time. My place. My bed. Less than half the time... And you can guess who orchestrated that...

Jimmy picks up the remote and pauses *Gladiator*. The four of us turn to him.

"It just isn't right, you know," he says.

"What isn't right?" says Stella, eyes expectant, chest out.

There's something going on there, you know. Something is rotten in Denmark. Something sexual. I took him in for getting guilty for getting sexual with his girl. Now he's paying me back, like for like—or almost, and certainly given time.

"Glad you asked, Stella. You're always on the ball."

Stella blushes, her chest blushes, in between her thighs blushes. He's practically inside her. Christ, if I was half of half a man, I'd...

"A flavor of favoritism," he says, "plain and simple. That's what it is. That's what it is—and sorry for involving you here, Stella, but the truth knows no allegiance except to itself—"

"Amen," says Stella, her panties practically dripping and down.

"The truth is that it is immoral to invite someone into your home, under the umbrella of generosity, under the *guise* of selflessness, only to lord your power over them once they have entrusted you with their safekeeping. It's cruel, Huck, and we won't stand for it."

"What the fuck you are talking about?"

"The bedroom Rota, or rather the lack thereof. We are either equal or we are not. And if we are—which of course we are, because how could be not be—then we must all have the opportunity to sleep in the bed, in equal measure, and without prejudice."

I have never heard Jimmy talk like this. I knew he was an upper-middle-class Jew from the wealthy suburbs. But he has always talked black, acted black, wanted to be black. Only now, he seems to have forgotten all that, remembering instead his overpriced education, having dusted off his oratory skills... I do not like new Jimmy. Smarter, silkier, the new him beats me... And suddenly I get to sleep on the left side of my bed, then the right side, then two nights on the couch, one in the chair, then back to the left side of the bed, then the right, and so on, and so forth. Jimmy fixes the rotation so that it goes: Me, Red, Jimmy, Stella, Ed. With me starting off on the left side of the bed, Red on my right, Jimmy and Stella sharing the couch, leaving Ed on the reclining chair. The long and short of it is, this rotation—which Jimmy swears he assigned randomly—leaves Jimmy and Stella conveniently sharing the couch one night, the bed another. The sleeping assignments also ensure that I never sleep in the same room as Stella. I consider refusing to go along with it, or cutting his throat or stabbing him in the chest thirty or forty times, but in the end I just do what I do, and roll over and take it.

The days go by. With no knocking at the door. We are a self-contained unit. And there is no knocking.

Until one day—a normal day: a day of drinking, of talking shit, of taking baths, of ogling Stella—gets interrupted by a hard and mean and bullying rapping. "I'll get it," says Jimmy. He stands up, he brushes his hand across Stella's face, she giggles, he adjusts himself, he goes to the door. I wonder if he's fucked her yet. I used to fuck her. I do not fuck her anymore. She doesn't give me the bedroom eyes. She used to though. Not so long ago, but so long ago. And I want them back. And I wonder if that's possible. In my dreams it is. In my dreams lots of good things happen. To me, not to Jimmy. He makes out badly. Most of the time, he doesn't make it out at all...

Jimmy is at the door. He opens it. There is talking, although I can't make out the words. Jimmy comes back with someone, a man I do not know, a tall, wiry, eyesore of a man, with an unpleasant face and unfortunate bone structure. The man stares at me, his eyes are pinned, the man is high, the man is dangerous. I do not feel safe. I look at Jimmy. Jimmy looks at me. "Relax," he says—I think to both of us. "Take it easy."

They go to the kitchen counter. Jimmy opens a draw. He takes out his scales, his weed, he pours out an ounce. "There you go," says Jimmy. He hands over the bag, takes the money from the man's extended, bone-heavy, hand. He walks the man out, closes the door, comes back, and pretends like everything's fine. Like he didn't just sell weed out of my apartment.

"Jimmy?" I say, sitting up.

"Yeah?" says Jimmy.

"Tell me that wasn't what I think it was."

"That wasn't what you think it was."

"What was that?"

"That was that."

"Jimmy...?"

"Yes?"

*"Jimmy...?"*

He takes a big suck of air. (He takes more than his share.)

"That was me, Jimmy, a drug dealer, dealing drugs. Like good drug dealers do from time to time."

"Jimmy, this is my apartment."

Another big suck of air.

"Huck, that is incorrect. This is not your apartment."

"Jimmy, this is my apartment."

"If this was your apartment," says Jimmy, "why is it that you don't sleep in your own bed?"

*The fury. The fury. I get the fury. Burning me up inside... I keep it in. And I watch it burn.*

"Because you made a Rota, Jimmy."

"Ah. But I didn't. Equality made the Rota, Huck."

"Jimmy, I saw you write the Rota out."

"Yes, but equality deemed it necessary. I was merely the stenographer. That means—"

"I know what it means."

"Okay. So, since you follow the Rota, you follow equality, and since you follow equality there is no *my* apartment, there is only the collective— only sharing and understanding, and caring and loving."

And that's how Jimmy starts dealing weed out of my apartment. And since he is bigger than me, and better with words, and since I can't be certain that he's not right, I roll over. I roll over and take it.

And everyone falls in line. We all smoke weed. And with Jimmy dealing, dealing out of our home—*our* home—we all smoke for free. And that keeps everyone happy (except me). And everyone falls in line. Even I fall in line. I don't want to be the only one not in line so I fall in line as well... Ed even picks up a job and a job means a wage and a wage is something that Ed hasn't had. Not for a long time. And that makes him happy and loyal and eager. He is Jimmy's delivery man. When Jimmy needs something delivered or picked up, he sends Ed. And for that Ed gets two hundred dollars a week. Ed stops being Ed. He becomes the guy behind the guy, the number two man. Which makes Jimmy number one. And everyone smokes for free, so everyone falls in line... behind Jimmy. In a house of equality, Jimmy is the most equal, followed by Ed. Followed Stella. Followed by Red. Followed by me.

The place that was mine, then ours, becomes Jimmy's, becomes real busy. Once Jimmy puts the word out that he's moved to Wrigley, the knocking gets regular, gets all hours. There can be knocking at one in the morning, knocking at four, it doesn't matter—Jimmy's doesn't close: we are round-the-clock, twenty-four-hour, customer-friendly. "Closing would be bad for us," he says. "We have to stay competitive." Everyone—having fallen in line—nods, drone-like. So I nod too, because I don't want to rock the boat. I'm not stupid though—I notice that Jimmy has good psychology. He uses the words like "we" and "us" when really he means "me" and "I." There is no profit-sharing here. Jimmy explains that profit sharing is against the principle of unity. "Money-talk is designed to divide us," he says. "We can not let it."

Red and Ed are dead

There is no more Red and Ed. Red and Ed are done, they are dead, their friendship is smashed and battered and ruined beyond a fix... It was Red, tired of falling in line, that triggered the showdown (in all big things there is always a showdown, a defining moment). He'd had enough, same as I'd had enough—only he had enough about him to say so when he had... He pulled me and Ed to the side, for a bathroom conference, leaving Jimmy serving a customer—as Stella watched him, doe-eyed and duck-faced. She has a thing for muscles, that girl. She is not one for brains or wit or charisma or goodness—or even badness. She has an itch for power. It'll be the end of her—you watch, you wait...

*So there we were, in the bathroom.* Red puts his finger to his lips, turns the taps on—both bath and basin—flushes the toilet too.

"Listen," he says, "we need a shift in the paradigm."

Red never used to talk like this, not when I met him. But we've been hanging around Jimmy and Jimmy rubs off on you—whether you want the slime or not.

"What paradigm?" I say.

Ed looks confused. I don't think he knows what paradigm means.

"The status quo."

Now Ed looks angry.

"Look, what the fuck are you guys talking about? Paradigms and statuses quos? Jimmy is out there now, unprotected. That dude, that harmless-looking customer, could have a gun or a knife or a grenade—hell, he could even have a cyanide pill in the palm of his hand, just waiting for the chance to slip it in Jimmy's drink... Only I'll never know. And why? Because I'm in here! I'm not out there, like I should be. Protecting our livelihoods.

And why is that? I'll tell you why. Because you guys want to talk under a waterfall like some goddamn gay dolphins."

"Calm down," says Red.

"I won't calm down."

"Ed, you're my best friend—we've known each other a long time—so I've got to give it you straight—Jimmy is using us."

"What the fuck are you talking about?" says Ed. "I pick up a salary."

"You pick up chump change."

Ed doesn't like hearing that. He squares up to Red. Red doesn't back down. Red is old, in bad shape, with a bum leg—but he doesn't back off.

"You calling me a chump, Red?"

"I'm saying what you're making is fucking chicken feed." He points to the door, toward the kitchen. "You have any idea how much business comes through these doors in an average week? I do. Because I've been keeping notes. The last four weeks I've written down everything that's been sold. I also heard Jimmy on the phone, agreeing on a price per kilo—so I know how much profit he makes per gram. I multiplied that by the number of grams he sells in a week. And the numbers are astounding. And what do you make off of that? Two hundred dollars a week. For being his errand boy. For taking all the risks, running around Chicago like an idiot with ounces stuffed in your underwears."

*Smack.* Ed slaps Red across the face with his fist. Ed is wearing a ring, a present from Jimmy, and it cuts a line of blood across Red's cheek. Red smiles.

"You're telling me that while we're conducting illegal businesses—businesses that could get us locked up in prison—you're busy taking notes for the prosecution? Is that what you're telling me?"

Red doesn't say anything. He wipes the blood away from his cheek and keeps on smiling.

Five becomes four

They stand, tall and upright, inches apart, breath on breath, and breathing hard. There is a violence in the air between them. I can taste it... No one blinks. I've noticed that—that they know how to stare without batting their lashes... I first saw it (the blinkless stare) in a movie. I was five or six or seven at the time. So I hadn't lost all my confidence, yet. And I remember thinking: I could do that. So I practiced. But my eyes didn't work like I wanted. Like Anthony Hopkins' eyes. And I got waterworks instead... Red is shaken. A tear drops from his left eye. I watch as it rolls down his cheek, trails through the crevices, falls under his chin. It leaves a path, a stain, illuminated by the bulb overhead... I am stunned. Ed hit Red. He hit his best friend. And right in front of me. And I did nothing. And I don't know what to do. I know what I *should* have done. I should have killed Ed the moment he put his hands on him. But I didn't. Now the moment's gone, and I'll never get it back. Even if I killed him now—even if I strangled him to the underground—it would be too little. It would still be a hesitated murder—not a pure friendship, not a proper gift... No one does anything. For a very long time all is suspended. Then it's over. Ed opens the door, turns the corner, and leaves us standing in the bathroom... I cannot look at Red.

"Look at me," he says.

I cannot, I do not. I stare at my feet.

"Look at me," he repeats. "It's not your fault."

"Red," my voice is choked and whisper-quiet, "I'm fucking sorry. I don't know why—"

"People freeze. It's not your fault."

"Listen," I say, my voice heading up the rungs to its usual volume, "if you want me to go in there now and—"

"Leave it alone," says Red.

"Because I would you know," I say. "I'd go in there and—"

Red puts his hand on my shoulder, and shakes his head.

"I need some air, kid. I'm going for a walk."

"Okay," I say, "then I'll come with you."

"No. You stay here." Red still has his hand on my shoulder. He squeezes. "You're a good kid."

I sit on my bed, alone, I drink, I wait, I watch the time. Jimmy and Ed and Stella are watching movies in the other room. They are watching something funny. I can tell because they are laughing. I stick my headphones on, I drown them out. I stare at the clock, at the hands, I will them round... One hour goes by, and another, and another. The hours keep passing until it's dark... I get worried about Red. He hasn't come back. He is my only friend and he is missing... I go into the other room. They are talking. But when I walk in they go quiet. I was going to ask them to help— to help me look for Red—but something tells me Ed's been talking, and Red's not welcome here anymore. By the looks on their faces, neither am I... I leave the apartment. I check the 7-Eleven, the pizza shop, the DVD store, the alleyway. When I don't find him there, I walk up toward Wrigley Field. I stop in at all the bars, I scan all the faces. I check all the alleyways up around Wrigleyville. I see blowjobs and dope deals, drunks and whores and crackheads. But no Red... I give up. At two in the morning, I go home... It is my turn on the couch tonight. But Jimmy is entertaining guests (people I do not know)—and the couch is being used. When I walk in, everyone stops talking. I say hello and no one answers—not even Stella. So I go to the bedroom and climb into bed. I am exhausted and, despite the loudness, I pass out immediately...

Ed wakes me up.

"Jimmy says you're not on Rota for the bed tonight. Huck, you need to be careful. You can't just go sleeping wherever you like. It's not good for the collective. It's not good for you."

I tell Ed I am sorry, and he shakes his head and he pulls me to my feet. I go into the kitchen. I lie across the tile, in between the sink and the bin. I do not have a pillow or a cover and the tile is cold and the air is cold and I am cold. I stand up and pour myself a pint of whiskey and drink as much of it as I can in one go. I manage about half, then I lie back down on the floor... The last thing I see is a cockroach. It stares at me. It looks sad.

I feel something run across my face. Tiny. Little. Legs. It wakes me up. The tile is cool and hard and sticky and wet. My head hurts, my back hurts, my arms and legs hurt. Everything cries. And more than before... There's something brewing. It is in my chest. I can tell because I've stopped coughing. That's a bad sign. My lungs are too weak to vibrate. I am frightened... I see the pint of whiskey, half empty, on the floor to my left. I sit upright. I reach, I hold, I carry, I drink. I take it down in one long burn. I feel worse. There is no warm packaging for me. That's my liver packing up... I put my head back down on the tile. I close my eyes and try to go back to sleep. I cannot. Instead I think about cockroaches... Eventually I get up, fill the sink with icy cold water and dunk my head. I make a slow ten count. When I come up I am dizzy and jolted and the room is spinning... I remember Red. I look around. He is not here. I have a bad feeling. I put on my shoes, I exit the apartment, I reach the elevator, the door opens. Mrs. Lipton steps out. I don't have time for it, not today, so I give her the tight nod, then try to squeeze past. She puts her hand on my chest.

"Can we talk for a minute?" she says.

"I can't, Mrs. Lipton. I need to find Red. He's missing. I *have* to go."

Four bulleted sentences and I'm out of breath and feeling faint.

Gently, I remove her hand from my body. I expect it to recoil, but it doesn't. Instead it springs back into place. I look down at her hand. And watch it as I breathe. Watch its thin, vein-heavy, shaking web of bones and bruising hold me up. She has kept me alive, this woman. This woman, I realize now, and just now, and right this second, is family. Is my only family. Other than Red. I must go find him.

"You won't find him out there," she says.

"I know," I say, "but I have to try, right? I mean, he'd do it for me."

"No," she says. "I mean..." She hesitates. "Red's staying at mine..."

She goes pink. "On the couch, of course."

"Mrs. Lipton?"

"Yes?"

"I'd like to see him please."

"Red doesn't want to see anyone."

"But it's me, surely if you tell him it's me, then—"

"He said to tell you, if I saw you... he said to tell you..." She takes a big breath in. "I'm *supposed* to tell you that he's fine..."

"But he's not?"

"No. No, he's not. He's really very sick, and in terrible shape. My guess is he's probably going to die. But then again, people have come back from worse, so you never know..."

"What are you talking about?"

"Red is a chronic alcoholic. He's been living on the streets, eating out of trash cans, drinking turpentine or whatever passes for cheap booze nowadays, and hasn't seen a doctor in thirty years. How do you *think* he's doing?"

"Not too good, I suppose."

"You getting smart with me?"

"No."

"Good. Okay, so listen, we should go somewhere and talk. There's things he told me before he moved in, things he said he wanted me to tell you. He'd do it himself but he's too embarrassed."

Me and Mrs. Lipton, sitting in the Cubby Bear, sharing a pitcher. It doesn't get weirder than this.

"What are you staring at?" she says.

"Nothing," I say. "It's just—"

"Just what? Just because I don't get bombed like you doesn't mean I don't like a beer now and again." She takes a long slug and finishes the glass. She motions for me to pour her another. "Look," she says, "there are some things about Red that he... well... he wasn't entirely accurate with you about."

"Okay."

"What I mean to say is—the way he may have phrased certain... *elements* of his life, to you, could have left things... open to misinterpretation... possibly... or not."

Mrs. Lipton waves at a waitress and one comes over. It's the thin girl I fucked, who became the fat girl who rejected me (although she didn't, if you remember: not technically, since I was only being nice... because she was fat...). She smiles at me, and mouths an apology. I feel like letting her know, that I wouldn't, not ever, but I've got Lipton with me so I let it slide. Lipton orders some big bourbons and some chicken wings and another pitcher. No one talks for a while. We sit and drink and eat and watch basketball... After the game is over and the food is over and the beer is over and the bourbon is over, Lipton turns to me. "So, everything is cleared up?"

"I honestly don't know what you've said to me. So, no, I guess not."

"Right. I can respect that." She waves for the bill. "I suppose I could have been clearer."

"Want to give it another shot?"

"Look, everyone bends the truth from time to time. Can we at least agree on that?"

"Sure."

"Okay. And you've lied before—to give people a certain impression, correct?"

"All the time."

"Right. Then that's settled. Red never went to Vietnam. He dodged the draft. He says he's sorry for lying to you, but that he needs to clean up his side of the street," she hiccups, "if he's going to get sober."

"Get sober?"

"Yes. Didn't I mention it? Red's going to get help. He's taking himself to his first Alcoholic Anonymous meeting today... I'd drive him but..." She hiccups again.

We walk back, lazily dragging our feet, taking breaks for cigarettes and hot dogs and general recharging.

"He loves you, you know."

I'm eating and my mouth is full and I don't say anything.

"He honest to God cried when he told me about how he lied to you about the war. 'Huck will never speak to me again,' he said. Of course, I told him he was being silly, getting like old fools get, from time to time, and with whiskey in them... oh yes, he's been drinking like a fish from the moment he stepped through my door. He's drank me dry. Well, almost—I'm down to melon schnapps. After that I'm out."

"But you said he's going to AA?"

"What? Oh right, yeah... Sure he's going... or he said he is. Only, you can never trust an alcoholic. That's the problem with people like you." She points a crusty nail at me, stabs the air an inch from my eyeball. "Anyway. Whether he gets dry or not, he's not coming back, not to your drug den, that's for sure. He wanted to make that perfectly clear. Got it?"

"Yeah," I say, "got it."

And then there were four...

## The Stella move

I go back home to break the news. I find Ed and Jimmy and Stella, and some customers, in the living room. I wait for the customers to leave.

"Red is gone," I say.

"Gone where?" says Ed.

"Gone, as in left," I reply.

"Oh," says Ed—Red's oldest and closest and dearest friend. Then he turns away and carries on carrying on—bagging up drugs, counting money—like nothing just happened, like Red was nothing to him.

*And I get the fury. But it stays inside.*

"How sad," says Stella. "Did he say why?"

I look at her, down at her—she is sat by Jimmy's feet. Keeping his eyes fixed on me, he lowers his hand, his big palm engulfing her head, and taps gently. "We should never ask why. It is counter-productive. It is self-seeking and selfish. We should only ask what—*what* do we do with this new information? *How* do we proceed?"

"Well," says Stella, "... what?"

He doesn't answer straight away. Instead he smiles at me, and drums his fingers—tap, tap, tap... tap, tap, tap... tap, tap, tap... in three-beat rhythm. He owns her now, and he knows I know; the tapping, the smirk, the mocking eyes, they are him dick-swinging, calling me out... *And the fury again. But closer this time. Closer to the surface. Where I cannot control it. Where it frightens me.*

He sighs. "We need to take emotion out of the equation. We need to be practical. First things first—we need to sure up the sleeping arrangements. There's only four of us now so there's no need for a Rota. Me and Stella will take the bed, you and Ed on the couch... Unless Stella objects of course, and she'd rather share with someone else."

I look at Stella. And Stella looks at me. And Jimmy drums his fingers. And Stella doesn't say anything. And my heart, it hurts.

"Well, that's settled then. Good meeting."

The rest of the day is the same as normal. Lots of people running in and out, buying weed. Cocaine too. A couple of days ago, Jimmy started selling coke out of our apartment. A vote would have been called, but Jimmy has implemented a new rule: any decision that, by definition, is in the best interests of the collective, doesn't need to be voted on, as a vote could go against the greater good. Jimmy says that there's too much money to be made in coke, that it would be criminal to pass it up. Ed, whose pay has just increased from two hundred to three hundred dollars a week, agrees. Stella is on board as well. She has a heavyweight cocaine habit.

It is five in the morning, six days after Red's departure, and I find myself in the bathroom. I cannot sleep. I did more coke than booze will calm. I must have drunk a liter of vodka, yet here I am, on the bathroom floor, wired and sober and shaking bad. My mind is racing. I have a naturally mental mind and cocaine is not good for it...

There is knocking at the door. I hold my breath. I do not move. I am completely still... But my heart is racing. It is beating loud. Very loud. I curse my body. It will give me away. They will hear. They will know... The door handle rattles. Someone is trying to get in. It is locked. But they are trying. I hold my breath, but harder this time. My heart. Racing. Someone whispers. They are calling my name. It is a girl's voice. It is quiet voice but, I can tell, it is a girl that is calling for me... I open the door. Stella is standing there. She has been crying. Her mascara has run. Her face, her beautiful face, is smeared. I see pain. Lots of pain.

"I have to go," she says.

"Okay," I say, "can I come with you?"

She hesitates. My heart. Racing.

"Okay," she says, "but I'm going now..."

I am going to say something. I don't know what, but something. Only, before I can, she turns, walks, opens the main door. I look at her. She is going. Now. My heart. I pull on my shoes, grab my keys, my wallet. I do not have time to grab anything else. She is already walking. Walking away. Down the corridor. Toward the elevator. I close the door. "Wait," I say. But she does not. I run after her. She does not hold the elevator door. It closes. I press the button. I keep pressing the button. I press and press and press and press. Rapid finger jabs. And my heart. I open the fire escape door. I run down. Bolt down six flights of stairs. My heart. Racing. I feel sick. I run out into the street. She is in a cab, she is all the way in, only her right foot trails, waiting for her to drag it inside. I get to the cab, I put my hand in the doorway. If she closes it, my hand will break. I do not care. Let her close it. Let her break my hand. My heart. She moves over, she looks away, I get in. She is shaking. I am shaking... The driver drives away. And we are gone. Just like that. We leave. We become me and Stella again. Sat in the back of a cab—shaking from cocaine and adrenaline and fear and nerves—I grab her hand. And she does not pull away. And I will not let her go. I will not *never* let her go…

# Chapter 17

## I ask

I ask. (Of course I do.) But she doesn't say. In the cab, at her place, in her bed. She just shakes her head. Pulls away. Says she doesn't want to talk about it... For two days I push her to open up. I tell her that whatever it is, I can deal with it. That, whatever it is, I can help... On the third day she says that maybe I should leave. That pushing her to talk is making it worse. "Maybe you should go," she says... So I tell her that I'll stop asking. And she says I can stay.

## The things we dont

And time passes. Slowly at first, as we nervously adjust. But then days become weeks, become more become months. And we fold into the familiar...

And we do not fuck... I mean, we sleep together. But that's about it. It gets like we're an old couple, forty years in—we take books to bed, drinks, sandwiches (if we're hungry)—we ignore each other. But not like we're in a fight. More like we've said all that needs to be said—and now we're just comfortable in the silence... We smile at each other. On the couch, as we pass in the kitchen, in the hallway, in doorways, and on the stairs. We wink at each other before the bed lights go out. We say goodnight, then a quick kiss, close-mouthed, before rolling over and away...

And we do not fight... Nothing gets broken. No plates, cups, windows or jaws. No one gets hit. The police are never called. No one gets dragged away. Or needs a lawyer... In the beginning, it feels weird, almost boring. I'd always seen relationships as long, drawn-out fights, relief only coming when someone gave up, called time. So this steady, peaceful existence rattles me, at first. And I try to fuck it up. I act unreasonable. Just to get a rise out of her. But she refuses to get drawn in—she doesn't even raise her voice—and, since you can't fight on your own, I give up...

And we straighten up... We stop the coke. It is hard, and for the first week we buck, almost cave, almost call someone and score. But we don't... After that we stop the weed. The coughing we can handle. My cough is bad, and hers is worse—her little frame rattles and vibrates something rotten—but the paranoia the smoke brings becomes too much, and, after a long and nonsensical discussion, we decide to give it up... Liquor goes next. With neither of us getting that warm pleasantness necessary to offset the shakes and sweats, we have another discussion and decide to dry out. We swap spirits for wine. We still drink a reasonable amount, between three and four bottles a day each, but the switch does us the world of good, and the shakes boil down to a manageable simmer... During all this, we use Valium to ease any unpleasantness, but when we run out, we decide not to get more.

And we isolate. And don't. And isolate. And mix... In the beginning, especially when we're adjusting to our new liquor and drugs policy, we pretty much keep to ourselves... Stella doesn't have a house phone. She keeps her mobile off. So no one bothers us. Someone knocks on the door once, but Stella raises her finger to her lips, and we stay real quiet, until the knocking stops and there is walking away... We get a little restless from time to time. When that happens Stella will turn her phone back on, listen to a million messages, then make a few calls. Usually that evening, we end up somewhere—a cool loft, a cool bar: somewhere cool—drinking white wine or red wine or rosé wine, watching everyone around us hit line after line, shot after shot. We watch for an hour, two hours, we smile, pretend like we're having fun too—but we are uncomfortable and we leave. We tell each other that we don't socialize because, we say, people are boring. But that's not the case. I mean, maybe it is, but that's not the reason. It's that deep down we're afraid *we* are boring—that stripped of our excesses, we're dull and ordinary and beige and brown and gray and cloud-covered. And everyone will know—that they'll find out—if we don't keep our distance.

And we are falling. Or I am falling. It's the not having sex—we're still not having sex, still have never had sex since I moved into her place—that clarifies it properly. I get my sex drive back. Without my edges sandpapered off, I get the itch. And I want to fuck her. And I tell her so too. But she says she's gone off sex. And that she's sorry. And that she understands if I want to move out or at least fool around with other women. Only, I don't. As much as I want to have sex. The idea of having anyone other than Stella sickens me, actually makes me feel like throwing up, so I stay frustratedly faithful and happy with my lot. And I watch myself fall. Deeper and deeper. And we never talk about it—because we never talk about serious things (not that I haven't tried, or she hasn't tried, but we don't know how: no one taught us how)—but I hope, hope that she's falling, and like I'm falling, and just as deep, or deeper still.

## The Script

The pages are done. All one hundred and four of them... A screenplay should be about a hundred pages. That's what Stella said, before we started writing. And somehow, and by accident, that's how it turned out... We can't decide on a name. I like "Shelonda," but Stella says it's too ethnic.

"Not that I'm a racist," she says, "but you've got to look at this like a business: what sells, demographics, target audiences. Art," she says, "art is really very scientific—when you get down to it."

... It was the strangest thing... I'd given up on writing. Decided that it wasn't for me. That I'd tried and failed. Tried and failed and picked myself up. For more trying, more failing. And I was done with it, that's what I told myself, I was done with all the failing, so there'd be no more trying to write, not any more...

But then one day we're sat on the couch, and Stella starts talking about something or other—although for the life of me I can't remember what. Anyhow, whatever it was leads to us reminiscing: about how we met, The Drake, and finally the motel... We talk about the motel, about what a horrible place it was. *Was*: as if it doesn't exist now that we're not there anymore, now that we're safe... But it *does* exist. As does all the badness surrounding it: blocks and buildings and backseats of infestation... I remember Shelonda and her pimp, and the things he makes her do. Makes, not made, for I know it's happening, right now, as I sit here, on the couch, sipping wine, drowning in cowardice...

Cloaked in shame, I get quiet. I stop talking. She touches my hand with hers, I pull away.

"What's the matter?" she asks.

"Nothing," I say. *I did nothing. Nothing to stop him. And I am nothing. And she cannot know. Cannot never know. Or she will leave me.*

"Come on," she says, "what is it?"

And I am trapped. I know she won't let it go. She's not the kind to... So I tell her... I'd never told her about it. About what happened. About him and her—and others like him and her—that I saw on my liquor store trips. The things I saw, pretended not to see. The things I saw, and drank out, drowned out. The things I saw. The things I saw...

I say about how she'd been offered to me, for sale, a child, for rape, and how I'd said no, and how I'd done nothing, and how I was nothing... And I'm breaking down. And I'm telling her. Telling her what a nothing I am. And I am sobbing. On the couch. Where it's safe. And I hate myself.

"It's not your fault," she says. And she keeps repeating. "It's not your fault." And she strokes my face and she holds my face and she holds me and she doesn't judge and I know that I love her, love *anyone*, for the first time...

The crying, the sobbing, the consoling stops. And I write. I write the story that makes her pain mean something. I feel bad doing it, and I don't want to, and I don't, don't do it, not at first.

"Writing isn't doing anything about it," I say. "If I do this, that makes me as bad as the pimp. I'm just getting paid off of her."

Stella shakes her head.

"Getting her story out there," she says, "getting it heard—that's how you help. People need to know. So you need to say. Go on," she says, pointing at the computer screen. "Write."

So I do...

I do not know her story. *The* story. Shelonda's story. Only a snapshot. A taste from my walks, from my passing pretending-not-to-notice glances... So I embellish. To get her truth out, I create: characters, background, plot.

... She is twelve. A child. He took her from busy people. Parents who worked all hours, who didn't have time for eye contact. He talked to her like she was a woman. He used a soft, kind voice. He gave her the eyes she hungered for, the eyes he said she deserved. He made her hate her parents... made promises too, used grown-up words like love and soul mate... And she ran away. Moved in with him. To his house, for sex and drugs and addiction... then to a sleazy hour-rate room, to sell her body for him for anyone for cents... *As I type, my hands shake with the fury, my eyes stream down my cheeks, the poison feels like it's draining out of me, down the sides of my face, and away...* I hate the pimp. More even than I hate myself, for leaving her. Than I hate my mother for leaving me. Than I hate my father and his weak gene... I paint the pimp: strong and dark, coal-black eyes, no heart. I draw her shaking and glassy and broken and bruised... I make it like she can never get out... Then I get her out...

The story is about a man (a real man, not a man like me) who goes to a motel to write a screenplay... Only he can't because he's got the block. So he just drinks instead, in his room, on his own. Liquor store, room, liquor store, room... After ten pages of set-up, my character, Tobias, is on his way to the liquor store when he gets offered Shelonda... To cut a long story short, somehow, against all odds, this weedy, white, alcoholic bag of bones, through sheer force of will, snatches Shelonda away from her pimp, rescuing himself in the process... The pimp magically disappears in the third act: no retribution, no comeback, he just lets Tobias and Shelonda walk off into the sunset together, like: well, I guess you won then, and good luck to you both... The last scene of the movie is Tobias taking Shelonda in as his own, filling in the paperwork for adoption. The End. A feel-good movie. The girl is saved. The man is saved. Vigilante justice wins. It's a Hollywood ending... When I'm done writing, I feel empty.

"That's natural, honey," she says. "We sold out. Now, if we really had some balls we should have written it so that he starts up an affair with Shelonda, gets her pregnant, and then pimps her out—you know, keep the cycle going. Only, you can't sell that in Hollywood. Sex sells, yes, but there are limits, even in LA."

She has a point. Pedophiles are very rarely the winners in Hollywood. Except behind cameras... and desks too, of course.

... For the next few days we sit and bask. We take bubble baths together, drink great coffee, eat apple pie. We live the good life. We talk about who could play who. I like Johnny Depp for the writer, an unknown for the girl, Ving Rhames for the pimp. There's no way Johnny could take Ving, meaning that's how it's got to be shot. Rabbit out the hat, impossible tricks... That'll keep the money-men happy.

# Chapter 18

Just hold on...

Back of a cab.
Solo trip.
Radio playing.
Static.
Bad signal.
"Sorry," says the driver, "it's the area."
He switches the radio.
He puts a tape in.
Bob Marley.
"Please switch that off," I say to the driver.
The driver turns to me. "What? You don't like Bob?"
I do not answer
but our eyes meet
mine and the driver's
and he sees I am a serious man...
He switches it off.
Silence.

Only the sound of *the fury*, like a wave, crashes
against my ear drums, gets me dizzy.
My eyes close...

I think about what she told me
after I told her
that I loved her...

I told her that I loved her
and she cried
said she loved me too
but that she was scared...
And I held her
held her
and told her
that I was scared too
but that it would be okay
that
we
would be
okay...

and we tried
tried
to sleep together
—make love—
but we couldn't
because she cried
and more this time
and told me

about before
about that thing she'd refused to talk about
—the why of leaving my apartment—
so
suddenly
her legs shaking, body shaking, eyes vacant, back of a cab, as I held her hand...

New cab now.
Solo trip.
Stella
she is in the bath
washing her dirt off her.
She has no dirt
She is clean and pure and kind and perfect
but she feels dirty...
He has done that
poisoned her
broke her brain...
he has done that...
And she washes
I can hear her now, from the back of this cab, hear the brush bristles scrub and scrape her tiny alabaster frame, rubbing it raw
breaking skin
breaking her
breaking me...

I can hear him too
laughing

loud
Jimmy the Jew
my medicine man...

*I'm coming Jimmy*
*I am coming*
*Just hold on...*


First
Rumi
Milly
Lipton
Red...
then you

Just hold on
Jimmy
I'm coming...



Rumi

I do not go to the diner. The talk we're about to have is not diner talk... So I wait. I take the cab ride to her place. Pay the driver. Count time... I sit under a street light. She lives in a cheap part of town. And the street lights work and don't and work and don't and don't and work, like that, down the block, blacked out sections where bad bulbs got dealt, where God and the Devil dealt bad glass, where drugs got dealt, dealers offered refuge, shadows for shady business... I watch it all. Counting time...

At two in the morning she comes home. Her silhouette freezes, then slows, edging carefully toward mine. Her apartment got dealt the bad bulbs and there is no light, no protection for tired, wired, waitressing women... I call out her name. So that she won't be scared, so that she will know it is me, and that there is nothing to be frightened of. I call out...

"Rumi, it's me, Huck."

"Jesus, Huck," she says, "what the hell are you doing here?"

This is not the welcome I'd imagined, the one I'd hoped for. *Fuck.* There is no over-wide smile. No brush back of hair. No head tilt to the side, no cheeks shocked rouge. There is none of that. There is only stern surprise, furrowed eyebrows. Even in the darkness I can feel her frowning...

I clear my throat.

"I just want to say..."

But then I stop...

I don't know *what* I want to say. Only that I need to say *something*—to all the people I *know* I need to say something to. Before I can go and do and be done and do dead.

"What is it?" she says. She checks her watch, her frown gets deeper, she sighs. "It's late. And I don't have time for you... For *people* like you."

And I know what I have to say.
"You're right. Can I come in?"
"No."
"Just for a minute?"
"No."

"Okay." I clear my throat. I am nervous, my heart races, but good races—not drugs races or scared races. "I'll say it here then... Rumi—I was not a writer. I *am* not a writer. But something happened and I wrote it." And my heart is racing. "And it might be bad, and it probably is because I can't write, but fuck it, I did it, I finished it and that made me happy... And something else happened, too. Something else good. That put me into the ether. I fell in love, and for the first time..." And I can feel the fury calling me, calling my name. "But then I got sad, Rumi. I mean real sad. See, the girl who I loved, the girl that I'm in love with, got *raped* by someone I know, and in my house, and while I was there... and I didn't know, not until just now, right before I came here... and it's killing me and it's killing her and he has to share it, he has to take it..." I feel something on my hand and I stop talking and look down and it's her hand and I brush it off because it's not the hand I need. And I keep talking. "I have to go now, but I wanted to come and tell you that I am not a writer and you were right and I am sorry and that's all I wanted to say."

She doesn't beg me to stay. Doesn't tell me not to do something foolish. She just stares at me. So

I stare back. For a little while, a few minutes, long minutes, before I turn around and go... I hear my name being called, but I keep on walking...

I hit a better street, one with lots of cabs. I flag one down, then give the driver Milly's address.

## Milly

She is alone when I get there. So I go straight up. There is no awkward pause on the steps outside her block, waiting for the John to finish, pay, leave. No feeling like a coward when I do not confront him. Or like a pussy when I do, and get my ass kicked hard...

I hit the stairs two at a time, and bound up. My legs, my chest, fueled by unfamiliar purpose, forget their decay...

Her door is closed. I bang and bang, and bang and bang, until I hear groggy feet, dragging across the filth underneath.

A muffled voice.

The door opens...

*Fuck.*

I hadn't come before. Because I knew what I would find. Knew that I would find this. And that this would break my heart.

And my heart, it breaks. My face, slackened by sadness, joins hers, slackened by the main-line.

I look at her arm. Needle marks. She is gone. My Milly is gone. Is never coming back.

I should have saved her...

I try to speak. And nothing.

She turns, and using the walls for support, slips down the hallway, and back onto her money machine.

I enter her room. It is filthy. But not like before. This bad is worse. This bad screams. *It is over, and I know it, and I'm ready...* Used condoms, old needles, blackened spoons, lighters, all on the floor... And my heart, it breaks.

I sit on the bed, on crawling sheets. Then I lie down, next to her. With the back of my hand, I stroke her hair, her back, I touch her face. I hold it between my hands. I kiss her lips.

I say things to her...

I talk about my father. About the day after he left. About how she'd saved me. I tell her that I should have saved her back. And that I didn't. And that I was sorry...

I say other things too.

Private things. Things between me and her. And when I'm done, I wait for her to say something. But she says nothing. She is somewhere else and with the needle... I grab her shoulders and shake. And some of her comes back. Enough to mumble prices... She says she's sorry about the room, that she's having a bad week, that all prices are at half the normal. She tries quoting me for this and that. She is staring at me through glazed eyes, inches away from mine, and she doesn't recognize me, my face. She thinks I am a John and she gives me a laundry list of things she'll do and the money she'll do it for.

She is selling herself for pennies.

And I stream. As I hold her and rock. Back and forth. Back and forth. Holding her head to my chest. Stroking her hair. Tears falling. Heart breaking.

And I have to leave, and I cannot breathe, and I have to leave, and I leave, and I leave and I leave, again, and I know I should have saved her...


## Lipton

My apartment building looks unfamiliar. Like, it's not my home... I take the elevator up to six, my chest beating. The door opens. I step out into the corridor. The fear of an early showdown shakes me inside. I look left. And right. Nothing. I walk up to Lipton's door, and knock. I hear feet, old feet, padding tired and slow and toward me. I hear out-of-breath breathing, the metallic sound of locks unlocking...

The door opens.

Her face. Shock. Sadness. Smile...

And I'm being hugged...

She releases her arms from around my waist, her face from my chest, and holds my shoulders with her hands.

Maternal eyes meet me.

"Where have you been?" she says.

I open my mouth to speak, but she cuts me off.

"It doesn't matter," she says, taking my hand, dragging me inside. "Come in," she says, "come in." And I'm being led down the corridor, into the living room.

I sit down on the couch, cellophane-wrapped to keep it new. It is small—a two-seater—but Red isn't sitting, so I sit, and wait, as she fusses over me, making coffee and sandwiches, talking loud from the kitchen about nothing in particular.

I wonder where Red is. I'm excited to see him. Sleeping probably. He's old, and tired, and needs rest. I have half a mind to wake him up...

She brings out a tray. She tries to pour me coffee. But her hands shake and she spills it—all over the sandwiches—and she gets angry at herself, and I tell her not to worry, and I clean it up.

I come back from the kitchen to find a different Lipton. Gone is the smile, the maternal fussing. She is staring, but not at me. Staring at something in the distance, at something in her head.

"Sit down, Huck," she says. "I have to talk to you."

"Okay," I say, "but I have some things I have to say first."

"Okay," she says.

And I tell her.

What she means to me.

How broken I was after my father. How broken before that, from my mother. How she had been, and is, my mother, in my mind, even when I didn't want it, resented her for it, but needed it, needed her. Needed stupid things like her letters: just to know that someone cared about me enough to write.

"And I just wanted to tell you that, Mrs. Lipton, because, well, it just seemed like I should."

She smiles—a small, sad, tight-lipped smile. A tear rolls out her right eye, down her cheek.

"I didn't mean to upset you," I say. "I'm sorry... I'd like to speak to Red now... I have things I need to say to him. Important things. Is he sleeping?"

More tears. Not rolling. Pouring. Her face is wet. Her lip quivers.

"What is it?"

But I know. Already know. I have seen loss before. Felt it. Before.

"Red is gone," she says. "He died four days ago. Funeral was yesterday. I didn't know how to reach you. I'm sorry, son. I'm so very sorry."

I stay very quiet. Very still. *Red was an old drunk,* says my head, *and old drunks die.* But my heart isn't listening. And I feel a pain like when my daddy went... That big. That bad.

"I came into the living room, and found him dead on the couch, right where you're sitting."

"I had things to tell him... Things to say."

We are silent for the longest time.

"If it would help, then I'll listen." She holds my hand, squeezes.

"Red was my father-figure friend. He was difficult and angry and stubborn and manipulative and kind and loving and courageous and loyal. He was the best friend I had. I *ever* had. He was my only real friend... And I didn't give a *shit* about what lies he told... and I wanted to come and tell him that... tell him that I loved him. *Unconditionally*."

We stand, we hug, I lie. I promise to come back soon... I know my path. I know my future. But she is old and good and Christian and needs lying to.

## Red

The molecules in the air are heavy and hard. They bounce off me like boulders, taking me off course, pushing me from one wall to the next, making the short walk long and torrid...

I have the key. I have the key—but I want it done right. So I knock, bow my head, and wait...

The turning of the lock, the opening of the door, the shock on Jimmy's face... With my fear-paint on, I look up. Just for a moment, just so he can see the fear. Then I look back down at my feet.

"May I come in, Jimmy?" I say. "I was hoping I could get some stuff."

He hesitates.

I beg for him to remember me. As I was. A coward.

"Sure," he says, "come on in, but I'm pretty busy so buy what you're buying then get out. Can't have you hanging around, screwing with business... Say, how's Stella?"

He's eyeballing me now, trying to read me. But I keep it in. Keep the fury in.

"She's good, Jimmy. I'll tell her you asked. Say, where's Ed?"

"What? Ed?" he says. "He's on a run... Now," he turns to me, "what can I get you?"

"A pound is good, Jimmy," I say, "if it's not too much trouble."

He chuckles.

"Sure, kid," he says. "I can help you out."

He turns.

I don't have a plan.

If Ed had been here I don't know what I would have done...

I look around.

I didn't bring a weapon

and I'm angry about that now

but I don't have time for *that* kind of anger

only the other kind

so I bottle it up

and start scanning the kitchen for...

A long and serious knife
hits my eye-line
and calls me over...
I see myself walking toward it.
A quick glance at Jimmy.
I have his back...
I see my hand.
It grabs the knife.
It does not shake
It is solid
and righteous...
I see it now
see what he did to her
see it in my head...
and I let it out
and I set it free
and I let
the fury
go...
I see the knife
see it move
in and out, in and out
red, blood, blood, flowing, screaming
in and out, in and out
red everywhere
red is dead
red is dead
red, red, red, red. Red.
Everywhere...
No more screaming...

I hear the sound of metal.
I look down.
The knife is no longer in my hand.
The fury
no longer in my heart.
My heart is
calm
is gentle
is loving
is kind.
The fury
is gone...
I go to the bathroom.
I take off my shirt, my pants, socks, shoes
everything.
I wash righteousness from my body
watch
as it swirls at my feet
watch
as red says goodbye to me.
And I cry.

# If you found this in a cab...

Buy

If you found this beaten-up in the back of a cab and would like a new copy, it is available worldwide through Amazon. Readers in the USA can also purchase through CreateSpace (a company that supports independent writers) at www.createspace.com/4536865. This novel is also available as an e-book through Amazon, iTunes or Smashwords.

# With a little help from my friends...

### Review

This is my first novel. I hope you liked it. Word of mouth is crucial for any writer to succeed. If you enjoyed the book, please consider leaving a review on Amazon or Goodreads, even if it's only a line or two. It would make all the difference and would be greatly appreciated.

### Subscribe

To subscribe to receive notification of my future book releases, visit my website at www.omarhaboubi.com. You'll also be able to see actors read chapters from this novel, view my poetry, and visit my blog.

### Message

Feel free to message me – I'd love to hear your views. You can follow me on Twitter @omarhaboubi, get in touch with me on Facebook at www.facebook.com/haboubibooks or send me an email at omarhaboubi@gmail.com.

Made in the USA
Charleston, SC
29 April 2014